Thomas Macquoid

Pictures and Legends from Normandy and Brittany

Thomas Macquoid

Pictures and Legends from Normandy and Brittany

ISBN/EAN: 9783337328702

Printed in Europe, USA, Canada, Australia, Japan

Cover: Foto ©Andreas Hilbeck / pixelio.de

More available books at **www.hansebooks.com**

PICTURES AND LEGENDS

FROM

NORMANDY AND BRITTANY

BY

THOMAS AND KATHARINE MACQUOID

WITH THIRTY-FOUR ILLUSTRATIONS

NEW YORK

G. P. PUTNAM'S SONS

27 AND 29 WEST 23D STREET

1881

TO

ELIZABETH CLARKE.

DEAR ELIZABETH,

You suggested the idea of "Pictures and Legends from Normandy and Brittany;" and we lovingly dedicate the book to you, in memory of your true and life-long friendship for us and for our children.

Affectionately yours,

THOMAS & KATHARINE MACQUOID.

STANLEY PLACE, CHELSEA.
October 1878.

CONTENTS.

CHAPTER I.

PAGE

Breton Fountains—The Fountain of Le Drennec—" Catherine Cloär and the Poulpican "   1

CHAPTER II.

A Hunt for "White Bread"—A Breton Beggar's Story—" The Ferry of Carnöet "   9

CHAPTER III.

Quimper—Our Landlady's Aunt's Story—" The Two Neighbours of Quimper "   28

CHAPTER IV.

Quimperlé—Le Faouët—The Story of " The Miller and his Lord "   75

CHAPTER V.

Pont-Aven—" The Legend of the Rocking-Stone of Trégunc "   92

CHAPTER VI.

Auray—The Story of " The Bisciaveret "   .   .   .   144

CHAPTER VII.

PAGE

Vannes—" The Glover of Vannes "   156

CHAPTER VIII.

Dinan—The Duel between Bertrand Du Guesclin and Sir
Thomas of Canterbury—The Story of La Garaye.   . 162

CHAPTER IX.

Dol—A Legend of St. Christopher—"The Old Woman's
Cow "—The Home of Chateaubriand—Château Combourg—Vitré   183

CHAPTER X.

Avranches—A Brace of Characters—The Story of " The Pilgrimage to the Mount "   199

CHAPTER XI.

Castle of Falaise—Arlette—Honfleur— Old Farm-House—
Pont-Audemer—The Fourolle—" Beside the Rille "   . 246

CHAPTER XII.

Caudebec—Rouen—St. Romain and the Dragon—"A Waif
of the Woods "—Château Gaillard 295

LIST OF ILLUSTRATIONS.

Drawn by Thomas R. Macquoid.

	PAGE
CATHEDRAL, VANNES .	*Frontispiece*
THE FOUNTAIN OF LE DRENNEC .	2
FOUNTAIN NEAR PONT-AVEN	8
A BRETON CHILD .	12
A BRETON BEGGAR .	15
SPIRES OF CATHEDRAL, QUIMPER .	29
OLD HOUSES, QUIMPER	31
MARKET-WOMEN, QUIMPER .	74
THE BRIDGE, QUIMPERLÉ .	75
MARKET-HOUSE, LE FAOUËT	76
CHÂTEAU OF HÉNAN .	92
ANNIK .	94
GUÉRIK	103
BEEHIVES	109
THE BRIDGE, AURAY .	144
OLD WOMAN SPINNING	145
RUE DE JERZUAL, DINAN .	160
RUINS OF THE ABBEY, LÉHON	169
CHURCH, LÉHON	170

	PAGE
THE CHÂTEAU OF LA GARAYE	172
OLD HOUSES, DOL	184
CHÂTEAU COMBOURG	194
OLD SHOPS, VITRÉ	196
PORCH OF CATHEDRAL, CHARTRES	204
LA MERVEILLE, MONT S. MICHEL	236
BIRTHPLACE OF WILLIAM THE CONQUEROR	246
MARKET-PLACE, HONFLEUR	249
A NORMAN FARM-HOUSE	250
OLD HOUSES, PONT-AUDEMER	262
MARKET-PLACE, CAUDEBEC	296
GRANDE RUE, CAUDEBEC	298
AN OLD COURT IN ROUEN	299
MONUMENT S. ROMAIN, ROUEN	303
CHÂTEAU GAILLARD	319

NOTE.

Some of the stories in this book are founded on popular legends and traditions, and a few have been adapted from the tales told by the story-telling beggars of Brittany.

PICTURES & LEGENDS.

CHAPTER I.

BRETON FOUNTAINS—THE FOUNTAIN OF LE DRENNEC—
CATHERINE CLOÄR AND THE POULPICAN.

THE two distinguishing features of Brittany are its
dolmens and other stone relics of a prehistoric age,
and its ivy-grown moss-covered fountains. These are
indescribably picturesque ; they are usually found, like
this fountain of Le Drennec, embosomed in trees,
against which the deeply-coloured stone-work is well
relieved. From the joints of the masonry springs the
delicate lady - fern, and all around is a richly - hued
tangle of briers and brambles, and decaying leaves of
varied tints. Morning and evening quaint groups are
gathered round these fountains——white-capped, dark-
faced, Breton women, with brass or brown stone pitchers,
linger and chat beside the clear flowing water, while
sometimes a youth, or more often an old man with

B

broad-brimmed hat, and long flowing locks, looks on and sees them fill and carry away the heavy weight of water, but rarely offers to lighten their labour.

A great interest is attached to these fountains from the superstitious fears with which they are regarded. Formerly the Korrigans had unbounded power over these secluded spots, and they are supposed by the peasants to have created the fountains, as the dwarfs or Poulpicans are believed to have built the Dolmens.

But in these days a crucifix, or else that which the Korrigan detests even more, the image of the Blessed Virgin, is almost always to be found on the fountain, and although the fairy still visits the place at evening-tide, and combs her long yellow hair, mirrored in the water, she is no longer seen by day as a little old white-haired witch, with red eyes and wrinkled face. The Korrigan is tiny, like the rest of her sisterhood, and by night she appears under an exquisitely beautiful form, clad only in a long white veil wrapped closely round her. This fairy has a wonderful knowledge of the healing art, and gives charms, it is said, to those who believe in her. Every year, at the first burst of spring, she holds high festival beside her special fountain. There, on a cloth of dazzling whiteness, are spread ethereal dainties, and in the centre is a cup filled with a liquor of which,

THE FOUNTAIN OF LE DRENNEC.

so says tradition, a single drop gives omnipotent wisdom ; but at the sound of a human footstep all vanishes into space, and only the bent grass blades tell of the festival. The sight of a priest, above all, puts the sprites to immediate flight ; but woe to the unlucky mortal who comes suddenly on a Korrigan when she is either counting the hoards she stores in the Dolmens, or as she lies combing her hair on the soft grass beside her fountain. Woe, too, to the youth or maiden who flings a stone in the water in which the Korrigan has hidden herself, especially if it be on a Saturday ; on that day, dedicated to the Blessed Virgin, the Korrigan is especially spiteful.

This fairy greatly covets newly born children, and is skilful at exchanging for one of these her own hideous little Poulpican or dwarf. Souvestre and other Breton writers tell the story of one of these changelings :—

A Breton mother, named Catherine Cloär, went out thoughtlessly one morning, leaving her newly born infant, a boy, in its cradle near the open cottage door, without making the sign of the cross over it, or commending it to God's protection. A Korrigan happening to pass by, heard the baby crowing to itself. She looked in and saw a lovely, fair, blue-eyed child, and at once she coveted it. She snatched it up, and placed in the cradle her own little son, who was black and more spiteful than a cat.

Catherine Cloär came home, but, owing to the glamour thrown over it by the fairy, she did not at first see any change in her baby. After a time she began to wonder that the child did not grow, and was so full of spite and mischief. As soon as it was old enough, it was sent to mind the cows, and it used to fasten thorn branches under the poor beasts' tails, and then to laugh heartily when they ran wildly about.

The poor mother was in despair ; she could not understand why her son should be so small of stature and so great in mischief. Sometimes she would say to her husband as they sat together beside the hearth,—

" May Saint Anne defend us, but that child cannot be our son ; he has too small a body, and his wits are too sharp."

But Cloär only stretched out his huge hands to warm at the fire, took his pipe out of his mouth, shook his long hair out of his eyes, and finally spat on the embers, grumbling something in his beard ; it was his way of answering his wife, and it drove her past bearing.

It happened one night that the child was left alone

in the cottage ; there was a storm of wind and rain, and all at once some one tapped at the window, and a gruff voice said,

" Have you any beasts to sell ?"

It was the butcher of Vannes, and spite of the storm, he wanted to see if he could make a bargain. He was entirely wrapped in a huge blue cloak which covered him and his horse and also the calf that he had with him tied by the legs in front of him. The Poulpican peeped through the window, and all at once he saw the three heads —the man's, the horse's, and the calf's—which seemed all to grow out of one body.

He shut the window in a great fright, saying,

" I saw the acorn before I saw the oak, but I never saw the like of this."

The butcher went away astonished at such words from a child, and when he next met Catherine Cloär he told her what he had heard.

Her suspicions had by this time grown so strong that she resolved to make them a certainty. She went at once, while the child was out in the fields, and bought a hundred eggs ; she broke them all, and ranged the half shells in front of the hearth in a long straight row, till they looked like a procession of surpliced priests at the *Fête Dieu.* She had just finished when she heard the voice of the strange child singing quietly to himself, and she hid behind the door.

He came in, and when he saw the egg-shells he muttered—

"I saw the acorn before I saw the oak, but the like of this I never saw."

Catherine had no longer any doubt, and as soon as her husband came in, she took him apart and told him the story, and they both decided that the little one was a demon and must be killed. They went in and seized the little creature, and were going to execute their project, when the Korrigan, whose power made her aware of what they were doing, suddenly appeared leading à fine grown boy by the hand.

"Take your son," she said to the parents. "I have fed him in the Dolmen of Tir-Tarden on roots and cinders—see how healthy and bright he is—and now give me back my Poulpican."

"The belief of the peasants," says Monsieur de la Villemarqué, "is that the Korrigans are the spirits of native Celtic princesses who, having refused to embrace Christianity when it was first preached in Armorica, incurred the Divine displeasure. The same hope for which they steal children makes them very desirous of allying themselves with men ; this is shown in one of the most popular of the Breton ballads, *The Sire de Nann and the Fairy.*

There are two fountains at Quinipily near Baud, most picturesque in character, although not so rich in detail as Le Drennec some way north of Brest. At St. Nicholas des Eaux on the Blavet, one of the most quaint and primitive of Breton villages, there is a large and well-preserved fountain, wreathed with brambles and bright with ferns, which seems as if it might have been in existence in the days of S. Brieuc and S. Gildas, those two wonder-working saints who built their hermitage on the opposite bank of the river Blavet, the shrine of some famous Pardon or Pilgrimage.

Brittany is essentially a country of marvels and miracles, both in the way of saints—St. Corentin, St. Gildas, St. Ronan, and St. Guenolé, and others whose fame meets the traveller continually, either in churches dedicated to them, or far more often in miracles worked in their names, attested by pictures and legends—or in its wonderful stones, the Menhirs and Dolmens of Carnac and Loc-Maria-Ker, and other places ; for these giant marvels are scattered broadly over the province, chiefly in Morbihan and Finistère.

Many strange and pagan rites are still secretly practised by the peasantry, dyed in a double superstition, around those uncouth and ancient relics. Even over the traveller, after some stay among them, they obtain a strange and weird fascination—a fascination that seems to put him in sympathy with the reserved and primitive people of South Brittany.

FOUNTAIN NEAR PONT-AVEN.

CHAPTER II.

A HUNT FOR "WHITE BREAD"—A BRETON BEGGAR—
THE FERRY OF CARNÖET.

WE were extremely hungry—famished is perhaps a truer word —for we had started from Landerneau without breakfasting.

We wanted to see several places of interest near this pretty little town, and we had reached the inn so late the night before that we had not bespoken any provisions for our journey.

This morning when our vehicle—a comfortable-looking machine, with a good horse, a capacious hood, and a seat big enough to hold three behind the driver —came clattering over the uneven stones, our landlord and his wife were still asleep. We asked the name of a place to breakfast at, but both the white-capped staring maids shook their heads ; they could only speak Breton. We asked the driver, but his French was very bad, and he did not seem to comprehend what we said. One of our party understood Breton thoroughly, but she could only speak just sufficient to tell the ugly, sullen-faced fellow that we would stop to breakfast wherever he could find " white bread ;" for although black bread when new is eatable, it seems generally stale and sour, and in this state is most unpalatable.

Off we drove, first to see the ruins of King Arthur's castle of La Garde Joyeuse. We could only find a picturesque bit of gateway wreathed with ivy, and a sort of vaulted crypt into which one of us had nearly fallen. The driver was so long in finding out this ruin that we began to feel starved, but though we stopped at every place like an inn in the villages we passed through, the answer was always the same—a shake of the head—when the driver asked for "white bread." After that we tried to find the ruined church of Beuzitconogan, in which is the tomb of Troilus de Montdragon, but our driver either could not or would not get into the right road, so at last we gave up the search, and told him to drive on till we could find a place to breakfast in. It was now two o'clock, and we had grown so faint and sick with hunger that I believe, if the villages we passed through had looked less squalid and dirty, we should have been capable of sitting down humbly to a meal of sour black bread and cider. But our driver gave us no choice ; he had a good horse, though it was getting tired, and he drove on rapidly, while we felt cross with him and with one another, and lost all interest in the charming country through which we were hurried.

A sudden turn in the road, and we all gave a shout of joy.

We were in the midst of a much larger village than any we had yet passed through, but there was no sign of an inn except that over a squalid-looking shed, with a filthy pool of black mud in front, was written, "Ici on loge à pied et à cheval," with its Breton equivalent beyond.

But our driver, to our joy, did not stop here, he drove across the wide stony street to a long low house, in the window of which were some groceries and sweeties. We jumped out gladly, and followed the driver through the low-arched doorway into a large room with heavy black beams overhead, from which hung skins of lard, bunches of herbs, and bundles of crêpes.

A very pleasant-faced intelligent-looking woman came forward to speak to us. Clinging shyly to her apron was a lovely little girl about six years old, fair-skinned, with regular features and wonderful large dark eyes. Her head was covered with a lilac cap, shaped like a Phrygian head-piece, and fitting close in front.

The woman apologised and said her house was not fit for us ; she had white bread, but she could only give us bread, butter, and eggs.

"Capital!" we said, feeling ready to eat the eggs with their shells.

"How many shall I cook?" she said timidly, looking at the three famished faces.

A BRETON CHILD.

"A dozen to begin with," was the reckless answer; and she ushered us upstairs, first into a sort of village club-room, and then into a small bed-room, the walls of which were covered with photographs and prints.

Here she spread a clean table-cloth on a small round table, and on this she placed a good-sized loaf, a lump of butter, in shape and size like a man's hat, some black-handled knives and forks, and a bottle of claret.

That was the most delicious meal we ever ate. How good that bread and butter was! How excellent that claret and those eggs! We had boiled eggs, fried eggs, œufs sur le plat—I am afraid to say how many eggs we swallowed—and finally, our hostess reappeared with a tray, on which were three cups full of black coffee and a small bottle of cognac.

When we had finished eating we asked for the bill, and then our landlady, shyly putting her hands behind her, said she did not know what to ask—would three francs be too much?—she had never breakfasted gentlefolks before; two francs for the eggs and bread and butter, and one franc for the claret, and twenty-five centimes each for the coffee and the brandy. We paid it, marvelling at the modesty of the charge. As we followed her downstairs, she said an old woman had come in, who, she thought, would amuse us. She was a professed story-teller.

"But can she tell stories in French?" we asked.

Our hostess looked puzzled, shrugged her shoulders,

and glanced at our friend who was trying to talk Breton to the pretty little girl clinging to her mother's skirts.

"Some of these people have a wonderful store of ballads and legends," our friend said, "and the beggars always tell the best stories. The stories are better than the ballads, which are many of them modern."

We all went down the rough uneven stairs rather eagerly. Our good meal had given a fresh aspect to life, and we felt a new interest in the journey, which an hour ago had grown so pale and uninteresting, spite of the glorious sunshine overhead ; we felt ready for any amount of adventures.

At one end of the long, low, dark room was the immense open fireplace, and close in the ingle nook, on an oaken bench, sat an old woman. She sat immovable, without turning her head or seeming to be aware of our presence. On her head was a dirty white linen kerchief tied tightly under her chin, and projecting so as to throw a deep shadow over her cruel, malicious, green eyes ; her bodice and sleeves had once been black, but now they were green and rusty, and patched with other colours, while numerous chinks and rents revealed a still older and more faded velvet garment be-

neath, which hung down in shreds below her waist ;
her rough, dark skirts seemed to be dropping to pieces,
—patches had been sewn on them with yellow twine, but

A BEGGAR.

these were breaking away from the worn-out stuff,—
in front the upper skirt had been completely torn
through, and was fastened together by a huge brass pin.
A coarse blue apron was the least ragged part of this

collection of rags and patches, but it was flung on one side, as if to display the tattered garments it would otherwise have hidden.   Her brown hideous-looking feet were shod in huge sabots, bound with rusty metal bands ; her hands were brown too, but they looked powerful and well fed ; there was no starving aspect either in her baggy brown cheeks, which seemed pushed up by the singularly long dark nostrils.   Her mouth was a long line across her face, drooping at the sides, a slight lift at each corner giving a fiendish grin to the inscrutable face of this murderous-looking sibyl.

When our friend greeted her in Breton, she turned and looked at her from head to foot, then raising her arm, she displayed a greasy - looking wallet at her side, and patting it with her strong veiny fingers, she whined something in Breton, and held out her hand.

The hostess said that she asked an alms for the love of the Lord God and of Madam the Virgin, so we all put something into her outstretched palm ; then, without looking at us, she began a long prayer for blessings on us and on our journey, and on the place to which we might be going.   We longed to interrupt her, for we wanted a story, but our hostess and her children and the driver stood listening as if they believed the dirty old witch was inspired. All at once she asked abruptly, "Where are they going?" in a strong coarse voice, quite unlike the professional whine that had gone before. Our hostess told her, in Breton, that we were going to Quimper, and that, as we were strangers, we should thankfully listen to any-thing she might tell us about that city.

She shut her hateful eyes at this and shook her head, but our hostess drew forward a long oaken bench, and signed to us to seat ourselves.

Presently the crone raised her head, blinking her wicked green eyes till she looked just like an old cat.

"Kemper-Corentin, Kemper-Corentin." Her voice had a sort of nasal drawl as she repeated the words to herself. She shook her head again, and looked into the fire.

"We are going on to Quimperlé, to Pont-Aven, and to Tregunc," our friend said to her in Breton.

"Ah!" The hostess bent down over the old woman. We heard the words Kemperlé and Tregunc, and we saw her point to a cauldron suspended over the wood-fire on the hearth. The beggar nodded, thrust one hand into the pot and pulled out a potato. Then she proceeded to tear the skin off with her long black nails, and when it was skinned, she crammed it nearly whole into her mouth. Our hostess nodded and winked at us. "Wait till she has eaten it," she said in French.

"Maharit," the old woman said, looking at the little girl. The child seemed to understand her by instinct. She went up to the huge black table, pulled at the half open drawer, and came back with a dirty mug half-full of buttermilk. The old woman drank this greedily, drew her hand across her lipless mouth, and then began a sort of low chant, seemingly addressed to the fire. As she went on her voice grew earnest, but the words being Breton we could not understand them ; but afterwards, when our friend told us the story the old woman had related, we could feel how graphic the narration had been, and how completely in the telling she had identified herself with the distraught Guern and his lost love.

The Ferry of Carnöet.

THE river Laita, which leads from Quimperlé to the ancient monastery of St. Maurice, flows along the border of the forest of Carnöet, and through a long series of beautiful meadows. Clumps of pines. chestnuts, and other trees adorn the charming banks of this river, and offer abundant subjects to both poet and painter.

In some parts the banks are very lofty, and the trees completely overhang the water, so that under their cool shade the fisherman avoids the noontide heat and takes his siesta in comfort.

About a league below Quimperlé is the ferry of Carnöet. Some portions of the old château of Carnöet still remain, and tradition says that this building was one of the many residences of the infamous Count Commore (the Bluebeard of Brittany), who is said to have murdered his numerous wives.

On the banks of the river an old oak stands at some distance from the ferry, its almost branchless trunk leans far over the stream and looks as if it must fall into the water. It is a very ancient tree, and a weird legend is attached to it.

Many years ago there lived in the village of Clohars a young couple called Guern and Maharit; they were betrothed, and were to be married two days after the " Pardon of the birds," which, as every one knows, happens every year in the month of June at the entrance of the forest of Carnöet.

One evening after sunset the lovers came home

from a visit to some relations in the parish of Guidel ; when they reached the ferry of Carnöet, Guern shouted for the ferryman.

"Wait for me, Maharit," he said, "while I go and light my pipe at my godfather's cottage; it is close by."

The boatman of the ferry was a mysterious being who lived alone in a hut beside the river. Strange stories were told of him. It grew darker and darker, and Maharit felt timid at the thought of being left alone. "Do not be long away, Guern," she said.

"I will be back, my beloved, before you are in the boat," and he ran away. The ferryman soon appeared : he was tall and wild-looking, and long grey hair floated over his shoulders.

"Who wants me ?" he growled. "It is too late. Are you alone maiden ?"

"Loïk Guern is coming ; he has only gone to light his pipe."

"He must be quick then ;—get into the boat," said the ferryman impatiently.

The girl obeyed mechanically, but she was surprised and frightened to see the ferryman jump and push the boat off from the bank without a moment's delay.

"What are you doing, my friend ?" she cried. "We must wait for Loïk Guern, I tell you."

There was no answer, and now the boat reached the current, but instead of passing across to the opposite shore they shot rapidly down the river.

"Stop, stop, my friend, for pity's sake!" cried Maharit in an agonised voice. "We must go back; what will Loïk Guern say to such folly?" She clasped her hands imploringly; but the ferryman neither spoke nor looked at her, and the boat still impelled forward, descended the river more and more rapidly.

Maharit bent towards the shore. "Loïk, Loïk," she cried. The words died away on her lips, for she saw shadowy forms standing on the gloomy banks; they stretched their arms towards her with menacing gestures, and she drew back shuddering. She knew these were the spirits of the murdered wives of Commore. Maharit uttered a loud cry and fell lifeless in the bottom of the boat.

Loïk Guern lit his pipe, said a few words to his godfather, and hastened back to the ferry. But Maharit was gone, and the boat was gone too! He gazed anxiously across the river, and up and down its banks, now cold and sombre in the gathering darkness. There was no sound or sign of living thing.

"Maharit, Maharit," he cried, "where art thou?" From far away a cry came to him on the night breeze.

At that moment the boat disappeared round a turn in the river.

"Maharit, Maharit ; Père Pouldu," shouted Guern.

Suddenly, from amidst the tall weeds and rushes near the ferry, rose up the gaunt figure of an old beggar woman.

"You waste your breath, young man," she said. "The boat and those in it are already far from here," and she pointed down the river.

"What do you mean, mother ? What has happened to Maharit ?"

"The young girl is gone to the shores of the departed ; she forgot to make the sign of the cross when she got into the boat, and she also looked behind her."

"You are mad," cried the peasant impatiently. "Go to the devil with your old wives' tales."

He did not wait for an answer ; he set off running like a madman along the river banks in the direction the old woman had pointed out, waking the silence of the night with cries for his beloved Maharit.

"Come back to me," he cried, "come back." But all in vain.

At daybreak Guern returned worn out and weary to his village. He went to the parents of the young girl—to her friends. He asked tidings of Maharit of every one he met, but he could gain no news of her, she had not been seen.

He passed the next three days in wild despair, searching for his beloved in the neighbouring villages and through the forest. Towards evening, on the third day, he sat down on a rock beside the river, overcome with grief and fatigue. Suddenly the old beggar woman stood before him. He had not heard her approach ; she seemed to spring out of the earth.

"Well, my poor little Guern, hast thou found thy beloved ? hast thou seen Maharit ?"

"Alas, no, mother! May the good God have pity on me, I am heart-broken," he said with tears in his eyes. "Have *you* news of the sweet child ? Tell me, for Christ's dear sake ! Speak quickly, mother. We only waited for the pardon of Toul-Foën to become man and wife."

"I have told you all I know, my poor Guern. The child forgot to make the sign of the cross when she got into the boat, and she spoke and looked behind her, and this gave the cruel ferryman power over her, and he has taken her to the shores of the ' departed.' "

"Where is this accursed shore of the dead ?"

" Ah, my poor Guern, blaspheme not," interrupted

the old woman. "It is a secret from Christians ; it is the secret of the sorcerer Milliguet—he personates the ferryman ; he conducts the boat from this haunted spot, and loses many souls. Yes, he is powerful ; but those whom Jesus loves are able to overcome him—and the charitable are always blessed by God. I am only a poor old woman, Loïk Guern. I am hungry—I am very hungry."

"My poor mother," said the young peasant, "here is some bread—take it. I care for nothing since I lost Maharit," and he burst into tears as he gave her his black loaf.

"Thank you, Guern. Ah, what a good heart you have ! You are a good Christian, and if you do as I bid —and if it is the will of God—you may release Maharit."

"The Holy Virgin reward you," said the poor fellow ; and he looked up with hope in his eyes. "What shall I do, mother ?"

"You must first cut a branch of holly, and you must cut it at midnight, in the village of the Korrigans. You know where it is, in the forest underneath the spot called ' the Stag's Leap.' Dip this holly branch in the holy water-stoup at the chapel of St. Leger, then at dusk go with it to the ferry."

"Yes, my mother," said Guern, eagerly. "And what next ?"

"Be patient, my son." She raised her shrivelled hand warningly. "You must then call the ferryman. This fellow has sold himself to the evil one," she went on, "and when you have got into the boat, be sure you do not look about or behind you, for every night the banks of the river are haunted by the dead wives of Commore, and their cries and gestures will trouble your reason. You will neither see nor hear them unless you look about or behind you. You must tell your beads diligently, and above all you must make the sign of the cross reverently ; and when you have come to the thirty-third bead of your rosary—the thirty-third you understand—"

"Yes, my mother, yes," said the young man breathlessly.

"You must raise the blessed holly branch and show it to the ferryman, and then in the name of Christ command him to take you *living* to the shores of the dead. Miliguet will tremble at the sight of the holly branch, and his power will leave him, and he will obey you. Do you remember all I have told you, Loïk Guern ?"

"Yes, my mother, and what will be the end ?"

"I see no farther," she said. "I can tell you nothing more, my son. Do exactly as I bid you, and wait in hope for the end."

She disappeared as suddenly as she had come, leaving Guern full of eager hope.

At midnight, he found his way to the village of the Korrigans. Close by the Stag's Leap he cut a branch of holly, and then he went off to the chapel of St. Leger, dipped the holly in the blessed fountain, and earnestly entreated the aid of the saint.

The next evening at sunset he went alone to the ferry of Carnöet, keeping the holly branch carefully hidden under his long jacket.

"Hola! Père Pouldu, ferry, ferry!" he shouted.

The ferryman came, and Guern got into the boat without a word. There was deep silence, only broken by the plash of the ferryman's oars in the water. At first Guern began to tell his beads silently, but with fervour ; but by the time the boat had reached the middle of the river he was so overcome by the remembrance of his lost Maharit that he forgot his prayers and the old woman's caution ; he looked behind him, the string of beads slipped from his trembling hands and fell into the water.

Instantly loud cries resounded along the banks, and the boat, drawn into the current, turned and dashed down the river with frightful rapidity.

Guern roused himself, and remembered the holly

branch ; he drew it forth and waved it before the silent ferryman.

"Conduct me to the shores of the departed," he cried ; "take me to my betrothed." But in his agitation he forgot to say the word "*living.*"

The boatman took no heed ; the boat drove on. Then, with an impulse over which he had no control, Guern in wild despair struck the ferryman with the consecrated branch.

The strange man uttered a terrible cry—threw down his oars—and plunged into the dark water. Still the boat drove madly on—on—on! Guern could never tell how long—till it struck with awful violence against a rock and was dashed to pieces beneath a gnarled oak that bent over the river.

For years afterwards, at all the pardons of Clohars, of St. Leger and their neighbourhood, was to be seen a pale distracted-looking man who ran hither and thither among the crowd. He cried out piteously, while tears ran down his furrowed cheeks, "Ah, my friends ; ah, for the love of God and the saints, take me to the shores of the dead !"

The young people used to look at him with surprise and pity, but the older folk only shook their heads and said "It is the poor madman of the ferry ; it is Loïk Guern."

CHAPTER III.

NEXT day when we reached Quimper we wondered that
old Barba—for we found that her name was Barba
Keroës—had had no story to tell us about this most quaint
and picturesque of Breton towns. It may certainly be
considered the capital of Finistére, and seems to contain
in its aspect, its people, and their costumes, the very
essence of all that is Breton—la vraie Bretagne breton-
nante. Lounging in front of our comfortable inn on
the banks of the Odet we told our landlady about old
Barba and her stories.

"There are many tales about Quimper, too," she
said. "I suppose you know all about King Gradlon
and St. Corentin, and about Fontenelle and his attack."

Yes ; we had heard all these stories—in fact we had
grown rather tired of King Gradlon and the drowning of
Ker-Is, having heard so much about it at Douarnenez.

The landlady looked back at her room on the left
of the entrance. "My old aunt there," she smiled

incredulously, " is a true Breton, and she has some strange

SPIRES OF CATHEDRAL, QUIMPER.

legends; one, which I suppose is true, about the Cathedral, though it seems hard to believe."

"Why do you suppose it to be true?" I asked.

"Ah, Madame! it must be true—when you go to see our Cathedral—and I can tell you it is worth going to see,—in a side chapel on the left side you will be shown a picture that tells the end of my aunt's story. Come in, come in, Mesdames, and talk to her—she is as deaf as a post; but she can tell you her story in French."

We went in out of the sunshine and found the little aunt half-asleep in a low chair. She was a tiny, frail-looking dark-eyed woman; very clean and neat, but so shy and nervous that she formed a striking contrast to Barba Keroës. And she told her story in quite another manner; in a monotonous feeble sing-song that almost robbed it of all interest.

The Two Neighbours of Quimper.

CHAPTER I.

ON THE MARKET-PLACE.

LONG AGO, centuries before its two graceful spires adorned the cathedral of St. Corentin, Jehan Kergrist and Olivier Logonna were the firmest pair of friends in the fair city of Quimper. For Quimper must always have been a fair city; even at this distance of time, so

OLD HOUSES, QUIMPER.

much of the moss of a former age clings about its quaint
market-place ; on its tree-shaded quays ; its rivers

where old grey gabled and towered houses look down at their own reflections in the water below—and, chief of all, in its grey old streets—that it is easy to call up a picture of the past, more especially on market-days, when the costumes and language of the people who come in crowds from the surrounding country are little different from what they were many hundred years ago.

There is a market to-day, and Jehan and Olivier are chatting together as they stroll among the booths and stalls. Suddenly they stand still. The eyes of both fix in one direction, and each man is seemingly so interested in what he sees that he does not ask his companion the reason of the sudden silence that has come between them.

A tall lay Sister is buying cabbages at the vegetable stall opposite. She takes up first one and then another of the huge heads so like immense green roses, lays them in her flat palms and poises them carefully. Then she smiles down at her companion.

" Thou art no judge of cabbages, little one," she says, " or I should ask thee to see how much difference there can be between two vegetables which to the eye look the same."

There is a smile on her companion's face, but the smiles of age and youth are as unlike as the cabbages in question.   Sister Ursula's smile creases the corners of her mouth and wrinkles her sallow face, while the smile of Françoise Nevez dimples and makes her pensive face beautiful.

"Sister Ursula," she says playfully, "is it not so with men and women?   Some who look one as good as another are really quite different."

A flush comes on Sister Ursula's pale face.

"It may be so with women, my child," she says hastily.   "Of men and their ways I know nothing, God be thanked," and she crosses herself devoutly.

Françoise laughed ; but men being a forbidden topic and cabbages not specially interesting, she looked round in search of amusement, and she met the full gaze of the two friends.

She shrank from being stared at, and so bright a colour rose in her face that Sister Ursula saw it, and being much accustomed to the charge of the young girls educated at the convent of Locmaria, in a moment she had discovered the cause.

"Come, come, my daughter," she said anxiously, "it is time for us to go home.   Annik has all we want in her basket ; she can follow us."

She looked round at a stout, black-browed, bare-footed serving-maid, whose square-topped close linen cap, not unlike a sugar-bag, set off her red cheeks and showed her to be an inhabitant of Quimper itself; the cap was far less picturesque than some of the other headpieces worn by Pont-l'Abbé and Pont-Aven women, and also by those of the other towns and villages who brought their goods to the Great Square of Quimper on market-day.

But Françoise lagged behind—at last she looked back over her shoulder.

"Sister Ursula," she said shyly, "did you see those two youths near us just now?"

"Well, what of them? they are just like other men." Sister Ursula spoke sharply. She had looked on men all her life as incarnations of evil. It disturbed her that her favourite Françoise should waste a thought on such godless mortals.

"But one of them is Monsieur Jehan Kergrist; I am sure it is he. He used to come and see me at my godfather's, and we used to play in the garden together, and—and my godfather loved him dearly." She blushed again; she remembered that Jehan had always called her his little wife. "Yes, I am sure it is Jehan, though he is altered." She looked over her shoulder again.

"Come, come along, my child; we are late already." Sister Ursula's face puckered with anxiety. What would the Abbess think, or Sister Clara, the mistress of the novices, if she, Ursula, who had always been looked on as the best watch-dog the convent possessed, suffered Françoise Nevez—the fairest, and in expectancy the richest, ward of the community—to look after a young man in the market-place of Quimper? "Is the child in love?" she asked herself.

What love might be Ursula did not know; but she believed it to be a species of Evil Eye or glamour cast by men—always incarnations of evil—on hapless girls, whom it usually led to misery and perdition, especially if the girls chanced to be rich and handsome.

Old Marie, the sieve-seller, had loitered over a bargain she was making to watch the little incident just recorded. The young men stood near her, and she had noted the direction of their eyes. When Françoise looked over her shoulder at Jehan Kergrist, the old woman clapped her hands and laughed out loud.

"Thou art in luck, my son," she said to Jehan; "that backward glance was for thee." She looked mockingly at Olivier Logonna, who was frowning till his black brows met over his narrow blood-shot eyes.

"Silence, old fool," he said. "How can a blind old beetle like you pretend to say which of us Mademoiselle

Nevez saw when she looked back just now ?   That old dragon of a sister was scolding her, I swear."

" Holy Virgin !" Marie crossed herself, and Jeanne Pichon, who was haggling over a sieve, also crossed herself, and shook her linen-capped head vigorously ; " dragon is no name for good Sister Ursula.   Fie for shame, young man !   Are you a heretic, or has Satan himself taken hold on you, that you can so speak of a holy sister of the sainted Cross ?"

" Mind your sieves, you old crow," Olivier said savagely.

Jehan looked in wonder at his friend, and he pulled his arm to draw him farther from the gossips.

" Be quiet, Kergrist,"—Olivier looked still more angry.   " You will tear the braid off my sleeve with your violence.   Go, if you want to go," he threw his arm from him rudely.   " I am in no such haste to leave the market."

Jehan looked surprised, then annoyed ; but Marie's two companions began to giggle at the quarrel between the friends.   Jehan bit his lip and walked across the market-place to a gabled house behind the cathedral.

As he passed in through the low round-headed doorway, the light streamed into the shop, and showed its dark oak-panelled walls and carved presses full of merchandise. An inner door facing the entrance stood open and revealed the massive staircase pillar with carved figures of saints guarding every landing, and a wealth of quaint masks and scrollwork between. The kitchen was screened off on the left from the staircase by a carved partition of black oak about ten feet high ; the stone walls on each side, except at the staircase opening, went up without any intervening ceiling to the skylight above. Jehan went on hurriedly beyond staircase and kitchen to a small richly furnished room. He closed the door behind him, turned the quaintly-worked key in the massive lock, and then sat down before an old desk and rested his head on his hands.

"I did not know it," he said sadly ; "and yet, now I think over the last few days, I might have known it— Olivier loves Françoise. What can I do? I would give my own life for him, and yet I cannot give up my hopes."

He covered his face with his hands, but he soon looked up again, and there was a smile on his honest face ; he was not nearly so handsome as Olivier—there was a heavy squareness about his features, but his eyes were dark and sweet.

"It must be so," he said. "I never saw him so moved ; he is always so staid and discreet. But I have loved her all my life," he went on. "I know it now, and Olivier has only seen her by chance—two or three times in the market-place—he has not even spoken to her, and he is always taken up with the last new face." He paused again, and a downcast look saddened his face. "It may be that Françoise would like him best ; girls are apt to like men who have had successes with women better than us simple fellows who only care for earnest honest love. But I will not be faint-hearted. Let us both try ; we are each rich enough to marry, thanks to the thrift and skill of our parents, and Françoise shall choose for herself. After all, I can but remain single for her sake—her happiness is the chief thing—sweet child."

CHAPTER II.

GODFATHER PICARD.

THE Abbess of the Convent of Holy Cross had risen from her high-backed oak chair, and was moving towards the door of her room. She stopped and turned round.

"Good day, Monsieur Picard ;" she bowed stiffly to her visitor. "As you specially require it, I will send the child to you, though you might have trusted to me to find out her wishes, since you consider that her inclination is to be studied."

The Abbess was a tall fine woman with a noble face, so pale that it scarcely seemed made of flesh and blood, but the smile that came with her words gave her a sarcastic, almost a cruel, expression.

Jean Picard's broad red face grew crimson, and his heavy brows met in a frown.

"Undoubtedly I do, Madame," he said sternly. "I married for love myself, and I never repented my act. Why shouldn't this poor little girl—as good as a child to me—have the same luck?"

"Luck is a false word, sir,"—her smile grew pitying, —"luck has nothing to do with the children of Holy Church. Good morning, Monsieur Picard."

She went out of the room, her thick woollen robes filling up the doorway as she passed through. As soon as the door shut behind her, Monsieur gave a sigh of relief and sat down in the Abbess's chair.

"She's a good woman, that I doubt not; but she has an eye to business," he said crossly. "She's not the saint my little Françoise makes her out to be. The Abbess knows as well as I do that Olivier Logonna is a richer man now, and likely to be in the future a much richer man than Jehan Kergrist can ever be, and she foresees that there will be more to be made for the convent out of Madame Logonna than out of Madame Kergrist; and, maybe, Olivier's handsome face and smooth tongue have had their way. Did she let him see Françoise, I wonder? Surely she would not venture without my permission."

The door opened, and in came Françoise Nevez; such a contrast with her bright face and golden hair to the pale, black-robed nun who had just left the room, that even to the prosaic old merchant, Jean Picard, it seemed as if sunshine had come into the room with his ward.

She ran up to him, kissed him on both cheeks before he could rise to greet her, and then put both her hands on his shoulders.

"What mischief is brewing, my dear godfather?— two visitors in one day is quite an event for Holy Cross, I can tell you; and you are the second gentleman who has come to see our Mother this afternoon."

Jean Picard grunted and looked very cross.

"Ah!" he said "who was the other?"

Françoise smiled and blushed.

"It was Monsieur Olivier Logonna."

"And what do you know about Logonna?" Picard spoke roughly. "You have never seen him at my house. What is he like, child?"

"Oh, I have seen him several times at market and in church, and to-day, when I was in the garden watering my flowers, our Mother passed by and presented Monsieur Logonna to me."

Picard grew red and angry.

"Well, and what do you think of him?"

The girl thought her guardian was jealous and tyrannical, and she felt inclined to tease.

"I thought a great many things," and she looked down demurely on the floor.

"Confound all women!" but Picard said this to himself—he looked awkwardly at his ward, and plunged his broad hand in among his hair.

"Do you want him for a husband?" he spoke so crossly that Françoise started.

"I never said so." Tears sprang in her eyes. "Why are you angry with me, godfather? may I not speak to anyone besides you?"

She had seated herself beside him on a low wooden stool, and as she spoke she stroked the back of his hand as it lay in his lap.

Jean Picard looked wistfully round the room, as if he expected some of the figures in the pictures that decorated the walls—a dark series representing the Triumphs of the cross—to come down and tell him how to manage his ward.   Jehan Kergrist had come to him that morning and had proposed for Françoise Nevez, and it had seemed such easy work to say "Yes," if Françoise were willing ; and now, instead of being able to plead for his young friend, he found that Olivier Logonna had been before him, both with the Abbess and with Françoise.

"Jehan has been a fool," he muttered ; "why did he delay? such a girl as Françoise cannot be hidden away—did he think no one had eyes but himself?"

"Come, come, godfather,"—the girl spoke half coaxingly, half pettishly,—"why may I not speak to Monsieur Logonna ?"

Jean looked down at her for a minute, and then he laid his hand on her golden head.

"You have not answered my question, little one. When you have done that, I will tell you what I think of Olivier Logonna."

"It is not a reasonable question, godfather," she pouted—then she looked winningly in his face. "How can I want a husband when I have you for a father ?"

Picard brightened with pleasure ; he bent down and kissed her fair forehead.

"Yes, my child, you must have a husband to take care of you, and if you wish for this Logonna you shall have him. He says he loves you, he has told the Abbess he does, and God forbid that I, of all men, should cross true love, even if it crosses my own wish. I had other hopes, but never mind them now."

Françoise flushed deeply and looked down. Picard sighed ; it seemed to him that this was her answer. She had chosen Olivier Logonna—what need to trouble her tender heart with the tale of Jehan Kergrist's love ?

He stroked her soft hair gently.

"Then it is settled, my little girl ;" he spoke gently. "I will tell Logonna that you will listen to him, and you must come home for the wooing."

He felt the head twitch away from his fingers, and Françoise rose up quickly.

"Oh godfather, what do you mean—why do we go on teasing one another ? Monsieur Logonna looked pleasant, and he spoke to me, but I could never marry him—never," she cried with emphasis.

Jean Picard looked helplessly at the pictures again. What did Françoise mean ? was there any hope for Jehan, or should he, by speaking of his young friend's love, ruin his hopes ?

"If Marie had given me any daughters," he thought, his face getting more and more perplexed, "I should then have learned how to deal with Françoise.   How am I to find out what this wayward child means ? "

Françoise had stood silently watching his face ; she was timid as well as impulsive, and it seemed to her that her frankness had vexed her good godfather.

She looked down at her pretty feet, and twisted her fingers together.

" Papa Picard ! " He looked up and the perplexity cleared away.   Ever since Françoise had been a toddling rosy child of three years old she had called him Papa Picard ; and now it seemed to honest, troubled Jean, that the reserve which her four years of convent life had brought into their intercourse had suddenly melted ; she was again his merry mischievous Françoise, the child he was bound to advise and protect, and who was to inherit his large fortune.

" Yes, yes, my little one ;" he rose up, put a hand on each of her shoulders, and kissed her forehead. " What does my Françoise want of her old father ?"

She blushed and hung her head.   " Do you then wish me to marry Monsieur Logonna, godfather ?"

Then she looked up and saw perplexity come back to his eyes and his lips, and she suddenly burst out laughing.   " Papa Picard, you want me to marry some one else," she said.   " Who is it ?"

Jean Picard took his hand from her shoulder, pulled out his handkerchief, and wiped his hot face.

"The Holy Virgin be praised," he said ; "my child shall not marry anyone she cannot love with her whole heart !" He stopped, then he hurried on : "If she can love Jehan Kergrist, Papa Picard would like her to marry him."

Françoise turned away quickly, and Picard thought she was vexed again ; she went up to the window and began tapping the small diamond panes with her fingers, while she gazed at some tall white lilies growing in one of the square flower pots of the convent garden.

Picard waited—but at last he grew impatient.

"I must be going, child ;" she turned round, and he saw that her cheeks were glowing, and her eyes had a sweet suffused look that was very like happiness. "Come, come, this will do !" he muttered, "you are getting on, Jean ; you begin to understand young girls!" then with a twinkle in his eyes, "I am then to say ' No ' to Monsieur Logonna, and ' No ' also to Jehan—is it so, my child ?"

Françoise screwed her lips together. "Suppose," she looked up brightly in his face, "you only do one message, Papa Picard ; I want to be so sure that Monsieur Kergrist is in earnest—that—that—he had better ask me himself."

CHAPTER III.

A TEMPTATION.

FOUR years have passed since Jehan Kergrist wedded fair Françoise Nevez in the cathedral of St. Corentin. It was a gay marriage, and the young couple had the good will and hearty prayers of most Quimper folk. Jehan had not hitherto had an enemy in the town, but his marriage had at first cost him his dearest friend.

For six months Olivier Logonna disappeared from Quimper, and when he came back he was a changed man ; he gave up all the pleasures to which he had been so much addicted, he never went into any company, nor was he often seen out of doors ; he spent all his time in his counting-house, or in making journeys connected with his business. At first he shunned his old companions, but Jehan's frank cordiality broke down Olivier's coldness, and soon the friends were to be seen crossing the market-place together as usual, and frequently in one another's shops ; on one point Olivier remained firm—he would not enter his neighbour's dwelling-house.

"I go nowhere," he said, and Jehan was obliged to accept the excuse.

He accepted it the more readily because Françoise

had a strong dislike to Olivier. When she found out that Logonna had known of his friend's long-cherished love for her, she could not forgive his request to the Abbess for leave to wed her.

"You are well rid of such a friend," she said to her husband ; "he cannot be honest."

"Hush, my child," Jehan had answered. "Olivier is one of the first and most highly honoured merchants of Quimper."

And so he was—his business went on increasing and increasing, and people wondered why he did not marry, for, like Jehan, he was an only son, and had lost his parents early.

Jehan Kergrist's affairs had also prospered, and he had two rosy little sons so like him that Jean Picard often scolded Françoise, and asked her why she had not bestowed some of her own good looks on her little ones.

But now, at the end of the four years, war broke out in Brittany ; towns were taken and pillaged, and property was no longer safe.

Jehan sat in his counting-house, with an open letter in his hand. It was from England, and it held the offer of a profitable undertaking ; indeed, the profits offered were so large that he scarcely felt justified in refusing the business. But yet he shrank from leaving his home at such an uncertain time of strife and blood-shed.

He would not tell Françoise—why should he lay on her his perplexity ? There was no one to advise him, his old friend Picard had gone to Normandy to secure some property he held there. So Jehan had to keep his troubles to himself, and he went about all that day with an anxious face and a troubled spirit.

He met Olivier Logonna in the market-place, but he said nothing to him. He could not confide to this friend that which was still untold to Françoise.

In the evening, just as he was preparing, in the homely fashion of those days, to close his shop with his apprentice's help, he met Logonna on the door-step.

" I want you to come and see me, Jehan," Olivier smiled genially. " I have shut myself up too long—I mean to admit my friends again, and I will begin with you, the best friend I have."

Jehan hesitated ; he knew that in their boyhood he had always told all his secrets to Olivier, and had received none of his friend's in return ; there seemed, too, a magnetic power in the silent Logonna which had always drawn his friend on to confidence, but he did not want to confide in him now. And yet if he told

Françoise as soon as he came home, why should he not ask Olivier's opinion? He hesitated again. Would Françoise like him to go and spend an evening with the man she so shrank from?

" Thank you, my friend," he said ; " I fear I cannot come."

" Then," Olivier looked very sad and downcast, " it is as I feared—you have never forgiven me, Jehan ; all your kindness has been a sham."

He turned to go away, but Jehan caught his arm.

" Stay—I will come. I will tell Françoise not to wait for me."

Logonna stopped him.

" Do not say to your wife that you are coming to me ; you can truly say you have business this evening, for it is business I want to talk with you."

Jehan looked unwilling—but he went back to speak to his wife.

Only the maid Gwen and the eldest boy were in the sitting-room.

" My mistress is upstairs with Conan," the girl said.

Jehan left a message for Françoise, and went back to his friend ; he was not sorry to miss seeing his wife.

Since his marriage Jehan had added many comforts to his home, and he was greatly struck by the bareness of Olivier's room.   The weather was cold, but there was no fire on the empty hearth ; and it seemed to Kergrist that some of the ancient carved furniture he remembered had disappeared.

Logonna was very friendly, but as soon as they were seated he suddenly said—

" Now, Jehan, what ails you ? have you made a bad bargain, or lost a cargo of merchandise ? something is troubling you."

His dark eyes glowed as he fixed them on Jehan's face ; the long and narrow gaze had the strange fascination of a serpent.

Jehan struggled ; he tried to withdraw his eyes from Logonna's, but he could not, and without his will his tongue answered : " Yes, my friend ; I have a trouble."

" Ah," Olivier sighed, but he kept silence ; he trusted to his eyes more than to his tongue.

Kergrist grew restless under the long narrow gaze ; he fidgeted and tried to look away.   In vain, his eyes came back and settled with an increasing expression of trust on his friend's face.

" It seems selfish," he began, " to trouble you with my troubles ; besides, I ought to be man enough to bear them for myself."

" That is not the teaching we get in church," said

Olivier ; " the sermon of last Sunday told us to ' bear one another's burdens.'"   He looked devout, and crossed himself, that his friend might see he was in earnest.

Jehan was puzzled and touched.   Olivier had never taken this tone with him before; it was rather the sort of reasoning he might have expected from Françoise.

" I will tell you my perplexity," he said at last ; " your wits are sharper than mine, and you will help me to see what I should do."   Olivier listened with fixed attention, but when Jehan spoke of the offer that had been made him, a fierce light shone in Logonna's eyes ; he checked this, and forced his lips into a smile of congratulation.

" You would have to be absent for some time," he said.

" Yes," Jehan sighed, " there is my trouble ; who can say what may happen to Quimper in two or three months, in seven or eight weeks even, and I might be longer ; am I right to risk so much for profit ?"

Olivier closed his eyes till they looked like two black oblique lines.   He sat thinking for a few moments.

" You say there is no time to lose," he said ; " you must go at once or relinquish the affair ; well, let us consider."

His heavy eyebrows met, and his lips closed tightly.

For a moment he thought he would make Kergrist give up the enterprise and snatch at it himself, so great was his greed for gold ; but this could not be done secretly, and he must not lose his character in Quimper for fair dealing.   Suddenly he looked up, his face aglow as he smiled brightly at his friend.   " I have it, Jehan ; you can do it safely.   Sell your stock and your house— you will easily find a purchaser—convert all you have into money, and then you can go away happy."

" And my wife and children ?"   Jehan looked angry. Did Olivier then suppose that he cared more for his goods than he did for his family ?

" Your wife and children will be safe with Jean Picard, and surely, Jehan, you will also rely on my devotion."

Kergrist looked unwilling, but he grasped his friend's outstretched hand.   " And the money, what can I do with it ?   In such times as these, whose money is safe ? I cannot leave it with Jean Picard, he is getting old."

" I will take charge of it," said Olivier.   " I promise you that I will watch over it as carefully as if it were my own.   Come, Jehan, trust my counsel ; be at rest ; a husband and a father has no right to lose such a splendid chance of doubling his fortune."

Chapter IV.

A TRAITOR.

A LITTLE way out of Quimper, beside the tree-shaded river, there was a pleasant many-gabled stone house, with a quaint round staircase tower at two of its corners. The wall that shut it in from the path beside the river was built of regular blocks of the same dark grey greenstone, and in front, between this wall and the house itself, was a pleasant strip of garden planted with quaint starry flowers and aromatic herbs. Behind the house, and on each side where the space was larger, were orchards with purple plums and rich brown pears ripening in the warm August sunshine.

Looking under the trees, you might have seen beyond them a plot of open ground, green and gold just now, with its crop of gourds and cabbages, over which a few butterflies still hovered, but over the herb-bed in front hung quite a colony of busy bees, filling the air with their soft humming.

There was a cheerful glow about the scene, and when presently two fat square-faced children, in long jackets and baggy breeches, came running out of the house, their merry faces and shrill outcries of joy seemed quite in keeping with the rest.

"Mother, mother," they cried joyfully, "there are more bees than ever to-day."

Françoise came out of the low round-headed doorway. She smiled at her children's words, but the smile faded at once from her pale face. She turned away and walked on till she reached the right-hand corner of the house, and then she went slowly into the orchard, her black dress and white cap in harmony with the green below and around her.

"Ah, my husband," she was saying to herself, "what can keep you from me ?—a year to-morrow since you went away—what can it be ?"

She had shrunk with a fear she could not give a reason for from her husband's undertaking ; but Jean Picard loudly advocated it, and offered so heartily to take the young wife and children to his home beside the Odet, that Françoise yielded when she saw that her husband really wished to go.

For the first two months she had from time to time received letters from Jehan ; then the war had extended from the frontier to the north coast of Brittany, and all tidings ceased. At last came a letter by a travelling pedlar, saying that Jehan had set out on his home journey; but this had come several months ago, and no news could be gained of him.

Old age was telling on Jean Picard; he had long ago given up business, but of late, since a slight illness, his health and mind had grown very feeble, and Françoise felt she could no longer rely on his judgment.

He had grown into a habit of consulting Olivier Logonna, and since he had become too feeble to go to Quimper, the rich young merchant came twice or thrice a week to the pleasant grey house beside the river, and sat for hours with Picard.

At first Françoise avoided meeting him, but one day, some time after Jehan's departure, Logonna surprised her sitting with the old man.

Olivier was so humble, so deeply reverent in his manner, he spoke so lovingly of her husband and of his return, that when he went away Françoise rebuked herself for want of charity, and resolved to tolerate Monsieur Logonna's visits. Jean Picard counted the hours till he came again, and referred the most trifling matters to Olivier.

The months lagged heavily by without any tidings, and Logonna came still oftener; Françoise was surprised one day at her own disappointment because he failed to come. She had few visitors, and it was a relief, after

the childish babbling of the old man, to turn to some
one with her anxious hopes and fears ; besides this, she
grew conscious of a strange power in those half-closed
dark eyes that drew her irresistibly to confidence ; and as
Logonna walked beside her under the trees, watching
the changes of her sweet loving face, he saw his power ;
his purpose strengthened—Françoise should be his,
spite of all her present love for Jehan Kergrist.

To-day beside the Odet he was busy with thoughts
of Françoise.

"My spies along the coast," he said, "are positive
that Jehan has not landed ; he is either in a French
prison, or he has fallen in trying to pass the frontier ;
he may have suffered shipwreck, or he may have married
an English wife."

He did not believe this last idea, but he tried to
force it on himself, so that he might impress it more
powerfully on Françoise.   He loved her too ardently to
be sure of his own influence.

"But even supposing the worst," he thought ; "if
Jehan comes back, he may have been plundered of his
gains, and then "—— he paused, a dark stern look, as if
the shadow of some evil being were reflected in his face,
changed him into a distorted likeness of himself ; "and
then," he went on with firm lips, "Jehan Kergrist is a

beggar, and Françoise will shrink from beggary; her own money belongs to the children, she cannot touch it, and she has always been used to riches; her ways and habits are delicate and soft, she could not endure privation or discomfort. No—Jehan the beggar will not be welcome, and—but I am a fool to waste thought on that which is impossible. Jehan must not return."

He urged on his horse, and soon reached the gabled house of Jean Picard.

"I will be careful," he said to himself; "no word or look shall betray me till my time comes;" and after taking his horse to the stable, he stole softly into the orchard.

When he came in sight of Françoise he stood still gazing. He was keenly alive to things of beauty, and the tall graceful figure, with its clasped hands and saddened face, made a picture of melancholy in vivid contrast to the glow all around, to the rich fruit smiling among the leaves overhead, and the golden light dancing in and out flecking the golden starred grass under foot, to the gay cries of the unseen children, and the soothing hum of the bees; he felt compelled to stand and gaze. Françoise was pondering his influence. "What is it that compels me to listen to him?" she said; "I believe in him while he is near, and yet the instant he leaves me I shrink from him and his words."

All at once she looked round and saw him so standing, with an eager look of excitement on his face.

She gave a little cry and ran towards him.

"You bring me news," she cried; "oh, tell it quickly!"

Her heaving bosom, her lovely eyes swimming with uncontrolled emotion, showed Olivier the hold Jehan yet possessed on her love.

He shook his head, with sorrow in his face and burning anger in his heart.

"I have no news that he is coming, my sweet friend. I have surmises, founded on my inquiries, it is true; but you will not listen to surmises."

She put her hand on his arm. "How do you mean? I will listen to anything that gives news of my husband."

Logonna turned away with a sad smile.

"Tell me," she went on; "I will know what you are hiding from me." Then she took her hand away and spoke more gently: "You must pardon me, Monsieur Logonna, but suspense makes me vehement and uncourteous."

She looked at him sweetly, he could scarcely restrain his love from showing itself.

"My friend,"—he kept his eyes on the ground,—
"you must pardon me if I give you pain. I have
reason to think that Kergrist will not return ; he is by
this time doubtless the husband of another wife."

Françoise grew colourless, then she flushed to the
edge of the matronly cap which hid her fair shining
hair.

"It is a false tale," she said sternly, "and you are
a false friend to repeat it."

" Pardon me," he hurried after her as she turned away,
and he spoke eagerly ; "you are very hard on Jehan.
What can he do ? if he marries and stays in England,
he will be rich ; but he has lost all ; if he comes back
here, he is a beggar, and he beggars you also."

She stopped and looked at him with a scared face.

"A beggar !—that cannot be—he told me he left
his money in safe charge in Quimper."   She fixed her
eyes earnestly on Olivier.

"That was his first intention. I had settled to
take charge of the coin, and then at the last he changed
his mind and took it with him."

Françoise stood very still and was silent. "He
could not be false to me," she said at last ; "he was
always true and honest."

"How patient, how trusting you are," Logonna

sighed. " My heart aches to think how such constancy is rewarded ; but indeed, dear lady, you waste it—you are certainly a free woman—either Kergrist is dead, or he is false, he is dead to you either way ; and yet, because I only try to show you the truth, you say I am a false friend. I swore to Kergrist that I would watch over and protect you, and it is surely part of this duty to tell you the result of the inquiries I have caused to be made. I have no doubt that Kergrist is at this moment happy with his new rich wife."

She turned on him passionately.

" You have some purpose in saying this—why do you do it ? Tell me that, too, and then I shall see whether I ought to hate you or believe you."

Her eyes glowed : she panted with excitement, and again she put her hand on his arm, as if to force the truth from him.

The pressure of her slender fingers maddened him.

" I have no motive," he said, with passion that equalled her own ; " but I love you more than my life. Can you not feel, Françoise,"—he gathered her hands hungrily into his—" that you are more to me than life itself ?"

She stood still, so shocked with surprise that she did not at once draw her hands from his burning clasp.

"What is any love you have known to mine?" he said ardently. "Can love that is fed by such love as yours compare with the fire of a heart that has been consuming itself all these years, its only nourishment regret? Oh, Françoise! give me at least a hope; do not drive me to despair."

She had drawn away her hands, and stood looking proudly at him.

"Monsieur Logonna, what you have just said I will try to forget; but you must not see me again."

Then she went swiftly round the angle of the house, and left him alone among the fruit-trees.

CHAPTER V.

"HE WILL RETURN," SHE SAID.

JEAN PICARD was dead—the funeral was over, and to the surprise of everyone, the notary of Quimper declared that the old merchant had left every liard he possessed, not to his beloved godchild Françoise Kergrist, but to his esteemed and trusted friend Olivier Logonna; who was also appointed guardian to the two Kergrist children, in place of the dead man.

This arrangement had necessitated more than one

meeting between the sorrowful Françoise and Logonna ;
but though he looked deeply penitent, she treated him
with a lofty contempt, and only spoke to him when
absolutely required to do so.

She was almost heartbroken to-day. The house
and all that it contained was the property of Logonna.
He had sent her a message through the village priest
of Locmaria, the priest who had married her and
Jehan, to ask her to consider herself as much mistress
of the house as she had been in her godfather's lifetime,
but she had refused. She saw that Father Felix
thought highly of Olivier, and she did not like to accuse
him, but she would not accept his offer.

"You will find it hard to live, my daughter ;"
Father Felix shook his head with deprecation. "Both
rent and provisions are dearer since the war began, and
you will find it hard to live in Quimper on what
remains to you."

"It will not be for long, Father ; Jehan must soon
come back now."

Father Felix shook his head ; Olivier had per-
suaded him that Jehan was dead, and more than once
the priest had advised Françoise to consider herself
a widow ; but she remained obstinate.

"Farewell, my child," he said ; "I hope you will

change your mind and stay here. I shall come again to-morrow."

He went out of the long low room, along a short clay-floored passage, but it seemed to her that he stopped halfway. She heard a cry, and then back came the sound of shuffling feet, and the priest's white scared face looked in on her again.

" Françoise," he spoke hoarsely, " my good child, prepare yourself: you are right—or it is his spirit."

" It is Jehan !" but she could not move : she stood with clasped hands and straining eyes awaiting her husband.

He came in. He was so grey, so wan and weary-looking—such a beggar in appearance, that he was scarcely to be recognised ; but Françoise took no note of this. She sprang forward and clasped him in her arms ; then she laid her head on his shoulder and sobbed out her joy and sorrow.

Father Felix stole quietly away to fetch the children He was glad that Françoise's sorrow was over, but still if she had been really a widow she might have married the rich man Olivier Logonna, and Olivier had promised a new shrine to the church of Locmaria. Father Felix was vexed with himself that he was not more entirely satisfied.

When he came back with the two children he was greatly surprised at the change in Jehan's manner. His face was red and angry, his eyes sparkled, and he was standing in front of Françoise, questioning her.

The little boys hung back shyly ; they did not recognise their father in this soiled, ragged man.

Jehan threw himself on a chair, and pointed at them angrily.

"They, too, take me for a beggar," he said. "Well, Father Felix, are you also in this precious conspiracy, to defraud me of what is really mine ?"

Françoise did not speak. She raised first one child and then another, and when she had placed them in their father's arms, she hurried to seek food for the wanderer. Meantime the children's kisses softened Jehan.

He turned more courteously to Father Felix who had begun to question him, and told him how he had been seized by a Danish pirate and made to work on board his captor's ship till he at last contrived to escape ; how he had been plundered of all he had, and thus had been forced to make a long journey on foot, and to beg his way from Bordeaux, near which place he had landed ; and now how his wife had greeted him with the news of Jean Picard's will, and also that Logonna had told her that her husband was a beggar.

"And are you not one, then, my son?" Father Felix brightened with a sudden hope. He had been in terrible anxiety for the future he saw for Françoise with this ruined husband.

"No, I swear by St. Corentin. No—I gave all my money, a very large sum, to Logonna, and he swore to watch over it as though it were his own, and to keep the matter a secret."

The priest gave a deep sigh of relief.

"And he has been secret, my son; even to me he has not said one word of the deposit entrusted to him."

"But I tell you, father, he has denied its existence. He has told my wife that I changed my plans and gave him nothing."

Father Felix smiled.

"Do you think, my son, he would tell a woman that which he concealed from me? It was but a pious deception to keep your secret from all. Olivier is a good man, and he has watched over your wife and children like a brother."

Jehan shrugged his shoulders.

"I loved Olivier dearly," he said; "but I did not think he would have juggled my wife out of her inheritance; he"——

The priest raised his hand.

"Forbear, my son. That was not his fault; the old man was childish and feeble; he grew so to depend on Logonna that he could not bear him out of his sight: he was besotted over him."

Jehan had grown calm and like himself, and when Françoise came into the room he folded her tenderly in his arms.

"My child," he said, "your godfather's will must be seen to. I will eat a crust of bread and drink a glass of wine—no more," he waved away the salver of good things which Gwen carried behind her mistress; "and then, father, by your leave we will all go to Quimper and find out the truth for ourselves."

CHAPTER VI.

THE ORDEAL.

THE trio took some time to reach Quimper. Françoise rode behind her husband on the old grey horse that had often carried her and her godfather, and Father Felix walked beside them. Before they reached the city gates the news had spread of Jehan's return.

The Bishop of Quimper sat alone in the Palace Library. At that time he and the Chapter of the Cathedral regulated the affairs of the city of Quimper, and, like a good captain, since war had broken out he had remained at the helm of public affairs.

A knock; the curtain which masked the door was drawn aside, and a servant asked an audience for Monsieur Olivier Logonna.

The bishop bowed, and then summoned a welcoming smile. He had no reason to dislike Logonna; Olivier was not liberal, but the priest of Locmaria asserted that he paid his dues, and led a good life—and yet the bishop had always shrunk from the dark-browed subtly smiling man.

"Good day, my son," he said, as Olivier bent low to kiss his hand; "what can I do for you?"

Olivier looked very sad.

"My lord, I am cast down with trouble. My fellow-townsman and friend Jehan Kergrist, whom we all thought dead, has returned—though, indeed, from what I hear, it is like enough that it is not he, but some impostor who has learned his story, and is passing himself off on the poor wife as her husband; if it be the true Jehan, then, alas, he is distraught and possessed."

The words jarred on the bishop; he looked up sharply at Olivier.

"On what do you found this charge?"

But there was another rapping at the door, and before the bishop had given leave the servant came in hurriedly.

"Pardon, my lord—but there is good news ; Jehan Kergrist is not dead after all ; he is waiting without."

The man had known Jehan all his life, and his eyes were bright with pleasure.

"He may come in ;" the bishop turned his head away from Olivier, who tried to interpose.

Jehan came in, followed by the priest and Françoise ; they all knelt and kissed the prelate's hand, but the bishop was shocked by the change he saw in Jehan.

Logonna came forward and greeted him.

"Welcome home, friend," he said ; "why, we had all given you up ;" he looked into Jehan's eyes, and Kergrist's doubts melted into renewed trust in his friend.

"I came to Quimper to find you, Olivier ; to ask you to restore the precious deposit I confided to you. I have lost all besides," he said frankly ; "that is to say, while this war lasts and trade is at an end with foreign countries."

Logonna looked at the bishop, and touched his forehead.

"My good Jehan, you mistake," he said gently. "Do you not remember what passed between us ? you gave me this precious charge, but at the last you changed your mind and I restored it to you—surely you remember that ?"

Jehan looked at him keenly, but Olivier met his eyes with a look of gentle pity in his dark narrow gaze.

"You are distraught, Olivier Logonna, or you are the blackest of liars. Recollect yourself; it was you who first urged this journey on me, and then you bade me secretly sell all that I had, and give you the money to take care of ; and I gave it."

The bishop looked earnestly from one face to the other.

"You are both men of good repute," he said, "and yet one of you must be a great sinner. Jehan, are you sure of what you say ?"

Spite of his secret shrinking from Logonna, the man's calm gentleness seemed to attest his innocence ; the angry face and impetuous gestures of miserable-looking, beggarly Jehan went against him in the bishop's mind.

"Oh, my lord, do not you doubt me," he said imploringly ; "I have no proof but my word, but I have never broken that."

"Did you take no receipt, then, for this money ?" The bishop's manner had become colder towards Jehan.

"No ; I would have as soon thought of asking a receipt from you, my lord."

The bishop sat musing; at last he looked sadly at Jehan.

"I must summon the Chapter, and you shall know the result of their conference ; but I must warn you, Jehan, that I fear it cannot be favourable to you. Till you went away, your good repute was equal to Monsieur Logonna's ; but you have been away for more than a year, and we do not know of your doings in the interval ; this will, I fear, go against you."

Françoise had stood clasping her hands on her bosom, but now she stepped forward and fell on her knees.

"My lord, we do not know what Jehan has been doing all this while, but a straight tree does not at once grow crooked ; until he went, his life had been spotless. Ah, my lord, no one knew how good he was but I." She paused to get courage.

"Peace, my poor child," said the bishop; "if Logonna had a wife, she would say as much for him as you do for Jehan. Now I must send you all away that I may consider this matter."

Françoise started up. "She could not say so, for he is not a good man," she cried with passion in her voice. " Ah, my lord, through this year you and others have seen but the outside of that false man ; he affirmed to me that my husband was beggared and had left me for a new wife, and he besought me to love him—him, Olivier Logonna ; traitor, you know this is truth !"

She almost screamed out the last words, and pointed at Olivier, who had flushed deeply while she spoke.

The bishop looked very stern. " I cannot enter into a fresh matter till the first is settled ; but if this is true, Logonna, it will deeply injure your cause."

Olivier had recovered himself. " I forgive her, my lord," he said quietly ; " no one can blame a wife's expedient to save her husband's credit."

The bishop seemed as if he did not hear ; he went out with a troubled look, but he bade Father Felix keep Jehan and his wife safely in a room by themselves till they were summoned to the Chapter-house. Logonna, he said, could return to his own house and hold himself in readiness.

The trial is over. Logonna and Jehan stand in the midst of the Chapter-house with the circle of grave faces bent on them. Most of the reverend judges side with Logonna, a few with Jehan, but these last are silenced, when all at once Logonna stands up and prays to be heard.

"Holy Fathers," he says reverently, " I am ready to swear by the Blessed Crucifix on the high altar that I restored to Jehan the money he accuses me of ; will the proof content you ?"

There is universal assent, and the bishop decrees that the oath shall at once be taken.

The procession forms, and slowly enters the cathedral from the long vaulted passage that connects the Chapter-house with it.   The church is full of the excited townsmen and women of Quimper.   Françoise walks as close as she can to her husband.

And now they stand before the high altar ; Logonna and Kergrist are side by side, and after some moments of solemn prayer, the bishop mounts the steps and stretches out his hands towards the crucifix ; presently he beckons Logonna forward.

Olivier turns to his neighbour : " Hold this for me," he whispers, and he hands Jehan the stick he has been walking with ; then he too mounts the steps of the altar.

"Swear," the bishop says, and there is a breathless hush.   The population of Quimper have thronged into the cathedral, but there is no sound ; in the deep stillness Françoise hears the throbbing of her heart.

"I swear," Olivier says—how feeble his voice sounds! —"that I restored to my friend and neighbour Jehan Kergrist the money which he says I received from him. I swear it on this holy symbol."

He stretches out his hand and touches the crucifix. Ah, what is that! the feet of the holy image loosen from the cross—a drop of blood falls—another, and then another.

Jehan's horror overmasters him, he lets fall the stick and reels against Father Felix who stands near him with Françoise. There is a chink of metal, and lo! the staff has broken, and from it has poured the stolen treasure, the precious deposit of Jehan Kergrist.

There is a pause, a deep hush, and then a groan rises from the assembled people ; the bishop waves his hand to motion Logonna from the altar which he has profaned.

But he stands immovable, and they seize him and drag him away ; he bursts into a shriek—he does not resist, but laughs and mocks at them with the gestures of an idiot. The awful judgment has taken away his reason.

In one of the side chapels of the fair cathedral of
St. Corentin there is over the altar the representation
of this legend and of the crime of Logonna of Quimper.

MARKET-WOMEN, QUIMPER.

THE BRIDGE, QUIMPERLÉ.

CHAPTER IV.

QUIMPERLÉ—LE FAOUËT—THE STORY OF "THE MILLER AND HIS LORD."

OUR next halting-place was at Quimperlé, perhaps the most exquisitely placed town in Brittany, at the junction of two rivers, the Elle and the Isole, hence its name Kemper - Elle, contracted into Quimperlé, for kemper signifies confluent. Below the charming little town the united rivers are called Laita, and on this is the ferry the scene of Barba Keroës's story. But the lovely river Elle winds its way through hills and wild rocky glens till it reaches Le Faouët, tempting the fisherman throughout its course with shady trout-pools, in which the fish seem inexhaustible, for even salmon are caught in the Elle. Beyond Le Faouët it winds round the base of the lofty rock, on the side of which perches the marvellous church of Ste. Barbe, and it was on our return from seeing this wonder—for it seemed to us one of the most curious attestations of a legend we ever had met with — that we heard the story of " The Miller and his Lord."

We had breakfasted at the inn of Le Faouët on our way to Ste. Barbe, and had been so content with the fare that we settled to dine there on our return instead of going on at once to Quimperlé; but when we proposed to order our dinner, the hostess—a pleasant-looking dark-eyed Bretonne—demurred : " There is table d'hôte at five o'clock," she said, " and there will be plenty to eat."

MARKET-HOUSE, LE FAOUËT.

When we got back, very tired and hungry, from Ste. Barbe, our company consisted of the host and two dirty-looking townsmen of Le Faouët, and the dinner was so very untempting that if we had not been afraid of the long drive in the dark to Quimperlé we should have ordered something else.

When we had finished, our driver could not be found, though we had sent word he was to get the carriage ready. We strolled out into the market-place and bought some pears and Breton buttons, and greatly admired the gold and silver ribbons which were for sale in company with some charming silk and velvet skull-caps for babies, embroidered with spangles of the most vivid colours.

This market-place of Le Faouët is very picturesque, a sort of double avenue of lofty trees, with a great market-house at one end.

Beyond the market-place, near the desolate-looking church, we saw an acquaintance we had made at Quimper, an old white-haired beggar, blind of one eye, and with a lame arm. As we came up to him he held his hat out without recognising us. But the first word spoken was enough.

"Ah," he said, "you are the gentlemen and lady who like to hear stories; come and listen now to this one of the miller who sold his wares in the market of Le Faouët."

A Legend of Le Faouët.

THE MILLER AND HIS LORD.

A GOOD many years ago there lived at Meslay—which village is, as you know, at some little distance from Le Faouët—a very poor miller. So poor was he that Michaelmas had come and gone four times without his paying the rent of his mill to the Baron his Lord.

The Baron went out for a day's shooting, and finding no sport turned to come home in a very bad temper.

What should he meet with on the way but the miller's cow, so he fired at her and shot her dead.

The miller's wife was not far off, and saw what had happened ; she ran home as fast as she could to her husband.

" Alas ! alas !" she cried, " we are ruined. The Lord Baron has killed our cow."

The miller said nothing, but he thought a good deal, and he resolved to take vengeance when the time came.

He skinned his cow that night, and as he lived some miles from Le Faouët, and next day was market-day there, he started off about midnight with his cow-skin over his shoulder.

He soon reached a thick wood, and he remembered that it was said to be the resort of a band of robbers. Such a panic seized him that he climbed up a tree and waited for daylight. He had not been long in hiding when he heard a noise, and soon the band of robbers stopped under the very tree he was in to divide their plunder.

By the light of a lantern they had with them, the miller saw a store of treasures spread on the ground, and there was a quarrelling and noise over it, the like of which he had never heard.

" Parbleu," he said to himself, " if I could only get hold of that money I should be a rich man," and suddenly he drops the cow-skin down among the quarrellers.

At sight of the horned head and black hide—for it was a black cow remember—the robbers thought Satan had come for their souls. Off they scamper as fast as they can, leaving their treasure on the ground.

"Well done you," says the miller, "that was a happy thought."

Down he scrambles out of the tree, gathers up the money, stows it away in his cow-skin, and runs all the way home.

The miller and his wife went on counting the money till daybreak, and then they gave over. It was quite beyond their arithmetic.

So next morning the miller bade his wife go and borrow a bushel measure from the Baron.

She went up to the castle and gave her husband's message.

"What can you want with a bushel measure?" said the Baron scornfully.

"My Lord Baron, we want to measure money with it."

"Money—did you say money? Do you dare to mock me, woman?"

"I mock you!—No, no, my Lord Baron, I am telling you the truth. Come and see for yourself."

So the Baron went home with the miller's wife, not knowing what to think.

When he saw the table all covered with crown pieces, he was beside himself with surprise.

"Where did you get that money from?" he asked, eagerly.

"I got it by selling my cow-skin, my Lord Baron, which I sold at the market Le Faouët, yesterday."

"Your cow-skin? Cow-skins are fetching a good price then."

"I should think so, my Lord, and you did me a great service when you killed my cow."

The Baron stared ; he said nothing, no not so

much as fare you well, he ran off to his castle at full speed, and gave orders to kill and skin every cow he had. Next market-day he sent off one of his men to Le Faouët with his cowskins,—there was a horse-load of them,—and told him to ask a bushel of silver for every skin.

The man rode off with the skins, and after a while he reached the great marketplace of Le Faouët.

"How do you sell your skins?" said a tanner, eyeing the load on the horse.

"A bushel's weight of silver for each skin," answered the servant.

"Come, come," said the tanner, "be serious can't you; how much a skin?"

"What I tell you, a bushel's weight of silver."

Another tanner came up and got the same answer, another, and then another, till at last all the tanners grew so angry, that they set upon the poor servant, beat him, rolled him on the ground, and took all his skins away from him.

When he got back to the castle his Lord came out eagerly.

"Where is the money?" he said.

"Ah, the money," the poor fellow scratched his head. "I know nothing about money, I only got blows and kicks at Le Faouët ; I am bruised from head to foot."

"The miller has cheated me," cried the Baron in a rage, "but never mind, my turn will come."

The miller cut up the dead cow and made a grand supper, and then he bade his wife go and invite the Lord Baron to come to it.

So she went and delivered her husband's invitation.

"How now ?" The Baron grew red with rage. "How dare you mock me again ; mocking me in my own house too."

She wrung her hands.

"Mon Dieu, my good Lord, how could I dare make fun of you ? Neither I nor my husband would venture to think of such a thing."

"Well," said the Baron, "I will come, if it is only to give your husband a bit of my mind. He thinks to outwit me perhaps."

So the Baron came and supped at the mill. There was quite a feast : fruit, and bacon, and roast beef. There was cider, and wine, and brandy ; never had there been such a spread at the mill.

Towards the end of the meal, when the liquor had been pretty freely drunk, and had warmed the hearts of the company, the miller said to his Lord—

" All the world knows how knowing you are, my good Lord, and yet, with all your sharpness, I wager you are not able to do what I can do."

" How so ?"

" I don't think you can raise the dead. Now I will kill my wife before your face, and then bring her to life again by playing the fiddle."

" I bet you twenty crowns you won't do it," says the Baron eagerly.

" And I bet twenty crowns that I will."

" Let us see it done, let us see it done," cry all the rest. " The Lord Baron holds to his wager."

The miller snatches a knife from the table, springs at his wife and makes a feint of cutting her throat, and she falls to all appearance dead on the ground, but the miller has really only cut a bladder full of blood purposely slung round her neck.

The Baron, too far off to detect the trick, was horrified when he saw the blood spout forth.

But the miller takes up his fiddle, settles it under his chin, and begins to play a lively air, and at the sound of the first notes his wife jumps up, and dances away as if nothing had ever ailed her, while the Baron stands gaping at her in staring wonder.

" Give me that fiddle, miller,"—he stretches out his

hand for it, "and I will let you off two years' rent for the mill."

"Agreed," says the miller, the bargain is struck, and the Baron hurries home in the greatest delight with the fiddle under his arm.

Going along he says to himself, "This is a clever thing I have learnt from that dolt of a miller. My wife is getting old, and by this means I can make her young and able to dance again."

He soon reaches home, and finds his wife sound asleep in bed.

"So much the better," thinks the Baron, "she will be none the wiser, good woman."

So he fetches a long and sharp knife from the kitchen, and cuts his wife's throat, and then he plays the fiddle, but he played and played till his wrists ached; the poor woman never even stirred, she was as dead as a sheep.

"What a fool that miller is," the Baron thought; "he bids me cut my wife's throat, and now, when I play the fiddle just as he did, she does not come to life one bit. He must have left out something. I must go at once and ask him what else I must do."

So off he ran to the mill; when he got there, he saw the miller in his shirt sleeves, holding a whip, with which he was furiously whipping a huge caldron which stood out in the midst of the mill-yard full of boiling water. The caldron had just been taken off the fire, but you see the Baron knew nothing of this.

"Holy Peter, miller;" he cried, "what are you about?"

The Baron was so surprised at this sight that he stood open-mouthed gazing at the miller. He forgot all about his dead wife.

"I am making the soup boil, my Lord. See how fast it boils."

The Baron goes close up to the caldron and looks at it with much attention.

"Yes, yes, I see," he says ; "and do you mean to tell me that your whip can make soup boil in this fashion ?"

"To be sure it can, my Lord. I do it to save wood ; bless your lordly heart, wood is much too dear and costly for the like of us."

"So it is ; you speak truly, varlet ;" then, stretching out his hand, "give me that whip, miller, and I will forgive you the other two years."

"A bargain, my lord Baron ; I give it to you."

So the Baron takes the whip from the miller and hastens back to his castle.

On his way home he says to himself, "And now I will cut down all my woods ; their sale will bring me in a heap of money."

And when he reached home he sold every tree on his land.

One Saturday evening the Baron's cook came to him with a sorely troubled face.

"My Lord," she said, "how am I to cook the dinner to-morrow? I have now neither wood nor faggots to burn, they are all spent."

"All right," her master answers; "do not you trouble yourself, cook, I know how to manage without wood or faggots either."

Next day being Sunday, the Baron bids his household attend high mass.

"Go all of you," says he, "men and women too. Grand Jean only will stay at home with me."

Now Grand Jean was very tall, and he was the Baron's chief attendant.

"And the dinner, my Lord," says the anxious cook; "who will get that ready?"

"Do not you trouble yourself, but take yourself off to church as I bid you."

So off they all start for the village church.

As soon as they are all out of sight the Baron says to Grand Jean,

"Bring the great caldron, and set it in the middle of the yard, and now fill it with water."

Then the Baron puts into the caldron fat and salt-meat, cabbages and turnips, salt and pepper,—everything, in short, requisite to make good soup. Next he takes off his coat and waistcoat, and begins to whip the water in the caldron with the miller's whip—but it is in vain—he whips and whips, and the water remains as cold as at first.

"My Lord, my Lord," cries the astonished Grand Jean, "what are you doing there?"

"Hold your tongue, fool, and you will see."

And Grand Jean stands looking, and the Baron begins to whip again with all his might. Every now and then he puts a finger into the caldron, but the water gets no warmer, and he begins to whip again.

At last he stops quite tired out. "Grand Jean," he cries furiously, "I begin to fear the miller has hoaxed me."

"He has certainly hoaxed you, my Lord," says Grand Jean, "there can be no doubt about it."

"Never mind, he shall die, and then there'll be an end to his hoaxes."

"Give him a sound taste of your whip instead, my Lord. Death is a heavy punishment."

"No, no! I tell you, nothing but death will cure him. Hoaxing me indeed — his lord and master!

Come along quick to the mill—bring a sack with you
—hurry along—we will tie the miller in the sack and
throw him in the great pond and let him drown."

Grand Jean shrugged his shoulders, then he threw
a sack across them, and followed his master to the
miller.

They seized the poor miller at unawares, and tied
him up in the sack, and then they hoisted it across
the mill-horse, for the great pond was some distance off.

As they went along, they saw coming along the
road behind them a merchant with three horses laden
with bales of goods.   The great fair of Le Faouët was
to take place next day, and he was on his way to it.
The Baron was greatly frightened ; he wanted to drown
the miller, but he did not want to be found out.

" Come along, Grand Jean," he cries ; " let us hide
behind the hedge bank out of sight till the merchant
has passed by."

And in a twinkle he and Grand Jean have
scrambled up the high bank over the hedge, and down
out of sight and hearing into the field beyond, leaving
the sack with the miller in it leaning against the bank
beside the road ; for the great pond is so near that
they have lifted the sack down from the mill-horse.

When the miller hears the trot trot of the mer-

chant's horses, he cries out, " No, I will not take her—
I will not take her."

At this the astonished merchant goes up to the sack.

" Hulloa," he exclaims, " what does this mean ?
who are you in the sack ?" But the miller cries out the
more, " I will not have her—no, I will not have her."

" You will not have whom ?" asks the merchant.

" The only daughter of a rich Baron, he is very
rich ; and he has only this child, and he is carrying me
off so as to force me to marry her."

" And is she really very rich ?" the merchant asks
greedily.

" Rich ! I believe you, richer than any one in these
parts."

" Then I will willingly marry her," says the merchant, eagerly.

" Very well, nothing is easier, you have only to
take my place in the sack, and she is yours ; only be
quick about it. The Baron will be back directly."

The merchant unties the sack, lets out the miller,
and takes his place, and the miller ties him up securely,
and then smacking the merchant's whip he drives the
baggage horses on to Le Faouët.

He is scarcely out of sight when the Baron and
Grand Jean come back to the sack.

"I will have her—I will marry her," cries the merchant.

"You will marry whom?" asks the Baron.

"Your daughter, my lord."

Now the Baron had no daughter.

"Ah, son of Satan," he cries; "go and seek her then at the bottom of the great pond."

And with that they took up the sack and flung it into the pond; and the merchant has not since been heard of.

Next morning the Baron and his attendant, Grand Jean, go off to the fair at Le Faouët.

They visit one gay shop after another; but all at once they stand still—they are struck with amazement —for there stands the miller of Meslay behind a counter spread with shining jewellery.

"How now, miller," says the Baron; "is it really you?"

"Yes, certainly, my Lord. You will buy some trinkets of me, will you not?"

"But how is it you are not in the pond?"

"Aha, you see, my Lord, I was not comfortable there; and yet I return you many thanks for my ducking, for it is in the pond that I found all the beautiful things you see here."

"You do not say so?"

"Yes, yes, I do. I only regret one thing, and that is, that you did not throw me a little farther in ; if you had done so I should have fallen among the golden trinkets, these you see are only silver gilt."

"Is that so?"

"As true as I stand here, my Lord."

"Then the golden trinkets are there still."

"Yes, at least I fancy so, but you must hasten if you really want to find them."

"Saint Fiacre ! this is indeed news," and off went the Baron as fast as he could, and off went Grand Jean behind him. They rode home, and then they ran to the pond. Grand Jean got there first ; he jumped in, and as he was very tall he raised his hand high out of the water to ask for help, for the poor fellow could not swim.

"See there," says the Baron, "he points to tell me to jump farther ; what a good fellow, he doubtless sees the gold farther in."

And he runs back, takes a spring, and jumps as far as he can into the water.

And since then he has never been heard of.

And this is the story of the miller of Meslay.

CHÂTEAU OF HÉNAN.

CHAPTER V.

PONT-AVEN—THE LEGEND OF THE ROCKING-STONE OF TREGUNC.

FROM Quimperlé we drove over to Pont-Aven, a quaint little town picturesquely situated on the river Aven. The Bretons often call Pont-Aven "the town of millers," there are so many mills on the rock-strewn little river.

Pont-Aven is a favourite resort of artists, French, English, and American, who lodge chiefly at the Hotel des Voyageurs, where capital accommodation is to be found. They seem to be "a happy band of brothers." At this hotel lived for a long time the clever American artist Robert Wylie. He received his art education in France, and his work is not much known in England, but his vivid transcripts of Breton life are well known in France and, no doubt, in his native country. To the great loss of art (he was at his prime of work) he died about a year ago very suddenly. His kindness to the young artists who visited Pont-Aven was very great.

The river Aven runs through a picturesque valley to the sea. At the mouth of this river stands the Château of Henan, a fine castle built in the second half of the fifteenth century. Rising above the trees that surround it, it is a picturesque feature in the landscape.

From Pont-Aven we went on to Concarneau, famous for its sardine fishing. On the way we stopped near the village of Tregunc to see the famous Rocking-Stone. It stands close to the high road, and is one of the wonders of South Brittany. The following wild legend is told about this huge stone, called "la pierre aux maris trompés."

The Rocking-Stone of Tregunc.

CHAPTER I.

ANNIK.

"MOUSSE, Mousse! Ah, but she's a cruel little beast; and yet, to see her, smooth as velvet, and to hear her purr, one would say, what a gentle cat is Mousse! Ah! but she is a cat after all."

The cat sat still, her black velvet-like coat glistening in the sunshine. Evidently she did not understand reproof. At Annik's words she purred more complacently than ever, without even a look at her pretty young mistress. Her green eyes were fixed intently on two large blue-bottle flies hovering about the exquisitely rosy flowers of a great oleander that stood in its green box outside the cottage door.

Annik shook her head at the cat, and then she crossed one leg over the other, pulled off her shoe and stocking, and began to examine her foot. It was a small well-shaped foot, and looked very pretty, just peeping from beneath her petticoat ; but, spite of the thickness of her leather shoe, the girl felt that a thorn had pierced it, and she gave a little cry of relief as she saw one end of the thorn still projecting from the skin. The wings of her snowy cap spread, as she bent forward, and showed glossy dark hair rolled closely away from her face ; her eyes too were dark, with long black lashes resting on cheeks almost as rosy as the oleander blossom under which she sat.

Annik was as pretty a little Breton maid as could be seen in Finistère ; and her costume was deliciously quaint. Her greenish blue home-spun apron hid the front of her skirt of darker blue, and reached quite to the bottom of it ; her charming winged white cap made exquisite light and shade on the sweet young face ; the bodice of her gown was black, as was also the inner body, which had long sleeves ; both were trimmed with black velvet, embroidered in lines of flame-coloured silk, and the square opening in front was filled with a fluted chemisette, ending in a frill of home-made lace round the slender throat ; below the chemisette her bodice was laced across with pale blue silk cord.

Something in the girl's appearance seemed out of keeping with the small one-storied cottage, with its overhanging oaken beams, in front of which she sat, from one of which beams, over the doorway, hung a bunch of mistletoe, signifying that cider was to be had within. Beyond the cottage, the road went uphill, and soon the sunshine, instead of shedding down a full stream of light, like that in which the black cat sat purring, asserted itself only in flecks and chequers of irregular design. For overhead, stretching across the road from the high bank on either side, as if to exchange greetings, were huge spreading chestnut boughs with fans of exquisite green leaves. A little higher up, the bank ended on the same side as the cottage, and a group of chestnuts stood on a wide opening of still rising ground. Here the light was yet more brilliant ; the dull yellow

of the ground between the tree-trunks seemed paved
here and there with tesseræ of gold, where corn had
been threshed in front of the great stone farm-house
that stood back among the trees. Opposite, on the
right, was a tall grey calvary, and the road sloping
downwards from this led to the church.

Annik took out the thorn, and just as she began to
draw her stocking over her pretty foot, a man appeared
at the top of the road coming from beyond the farm-
house. There had been no rain for several days, and
his tread was not heard at that distance on the dusty
ground. He came along with a lowering expression of
discontent, swinging the arm, which held his heavy
cudgel ; his large, black, low-crowned hat pulled over
his eyes. All at once he saw Annik. He stopped,
thrust his empty hand into his pocket, and gazed
earnestly forward. His wide mouth, open with surprise,
showed a range of gleaming wolf-like teeth. He re-
pressed the exclamation on his tongue, lest he should
disturb the picture below him, and stood still gazing.

Annik had left off talking to the cat ; she sat
leisurely putting on her shoe, crooning meanwhile a
wailing cradle ditty, as if the little foot were a baby,
and she were lulling it to sleep.

The man's face meantime had changed strangely.

As he came in sight you would have said that love and joy could have found no power of expression in his features ; now, as he stood gazing, pleasure at least shone out of his eyes, mingled with delighted admiration.

He had been too much absorbed to heed any sound, but footsteps had been for some minutes toiling up the stony road from the church, and now the tall bent figure of a priest, with his breviary under his arm, and a small bag in one hand, came behind the gazer. The priest, who was no other than the Curé of the village, looked intently when he saw a stranger, and then rapidly beyond him, to see what had fixed his attention. The Curé was very thin, with small, mild blue eyes, but he looked healthy, and the colour on his cheek deepened with vexation as he followed the strong dark gaze down-hill, and saw on whom it rested. He went on past the strange man, and then turned back and looked in his face—only to be seen by a direct front view, for the man's high shirt-collar hid the lower part of his features, and his long dark hair fell over his eyes and cheeks. The eyes were deep-set and unpleasant in expression. They scanned the priest searchingly ; then the man pulled off his hat, and gave an awkward smile.

" Good morning, father ; you have forgotten Lao Coätfrec, it seems."

The priest started, and then, while he returned the greeting, looked intently at the hard determined face. It was handsome, perhaps, as regarded colour and features, but there was no beauty of expression : the lower nature reigned supreme.

" Lao ! is it indeed Lao ?" and then the Curé stood silent. He looked disturbed and hesitating, as if he wished to speak, and yet was withheld by prudence.

Meantime Lao's eyes had travelled back to Annik. He said abruptly, " Father, who is the young girl beside the cottage ? I have been away so long that the young ones have grown out of remembrance."

Again the Curé looked disturbed. " You are not likely to remember that young woman, Lao ; she is not a Kérion girl ; she comes from Auray. Her aunt married the widower Guérik—you remember him at the farm here ?" He looked back at the stone farm-house. " His second wife and her niece, Annik, came from Auray ; and when the wife died, a year ago, the niece remained with Guérik."

Lao shrugged his shoulders, but his dark eyes gleamed with curiosity.

" I hope she has enough to keep her," he said carelessly. " Guérik, as I remember him, is not a man who would care to be burdened with a child who is not of his blood."

The priest was too simple to see Lao's drift.   His cheeks flushed a little as he answered—

"Annik lives with farmer Guérik because she is his niece by marriage, and because she is alone in the world.   She has no blood relations, but she has a good sum put by for her, and the prettiest little cow in Guérik's stable is Annik's.   One has only to look at her and see that she is no beggar : and she is good ; yes, she is very good."

His voice sank to a faint murmur.   As he ended, the good father suddenly remembered the admiration he had remarked in Lao's eyes.   He felt he was saying too much, and he wished he had not praised Annik or said a word about her money.

"And where have you been all these years ?" he said quickly.   "We heard that you had gone to sea ; you must have been away eight years or more."

"About that time, Monsieur.   I went to try the fishing, and then I heard of my mother's death,"—here Lao's eyes drooped under the priest's gaze,—"I went away to foreign parts then ; and to-day I have come back here to see my grandmother."

The Curé crossed himself.

"I am sorry to say your grandmother is not a good companion for old or young, Lao ; age does not mend

Ursule. She despises all that you were taught to reverence when you were a boy."

" That is a long time ago, Monsieur." Lao laughed. " I love the poor old woman ; she is all I have in the world to care for ; I am sure there is no harm in her ; but she is more clever than her neighbours, and so they are spiteful ; it is always so."

The Curé looked stern as well as grave.

" I judge no man or woman from report, Lao. I know that Ursule does not fear God ; and I warn you against her influence."

Lao laughed, and then he hitched up the broad leather belt he wore, and stopped in his walk.

" Good day to you, father. I must go and see my old gossip Guérik." And he turned towards the farm-house.

The priest went on with trouble on his usually placid face. As he reached the bottom of the slope Annik looked round.

She rose when she saw the Curé, and at her smiling greeting his face cleared.

" Good-day, my child. I am going away, but only as far as Concarneau ; so you will know where to find me if I should be needed."

" Going away !" Annik's eyes opened in wide

wonder. She had not lived many years in Kérion ; but she could not remember the day when she had not seen Monsieur le Curé.

" Is there any reason why I should stay at home, my child ? If there is, tell me ;" and he smiled.

"No ; oh, no! forgive me." Annik blushed with confusion. "The change will be good for Monsieur, but—we shall be all glad to see him back."

"And I glad to return, dear child." He put his hand on her head. "I have said I will stay till Saturday morning, but I may return on Friday—who knows? Go and see Jeanneton sometimes. Farewell."

The girl knelt down in the dusty road to receive his fatherly blessing. The Curé gave it, and then he passed quickly on his way to Concarneau.

CHAPTER II.

SILVESTIK.

" WELL, good-day, old friend ; it was a good chance that brought you back to Kérion; I will think it over. Leave all to me, and it shall go smoothly, I promise you."

The speaker, Mathurin Guérik, came to the arched door of his old stone house, and nodded farewell to Lao.

Then he smiled, and rubbed his hard brown hands together in congratulation of his own manœuvres. Guérik was short and broad, and his long red hair was

GUÉRIK.

not a becoming frame to his repulsive sullen face. His long half-shut grey eyes were twinkling with satisfaction.

"Nothing could have happened better. The girl says 'No' to every man I propose to her; and, indeed, there are but few to choose from in Kérion who have money. This one is rich ; I can see it even in his walk "—he stood watching Lao Coätfrec out of sight—" and there are no relations to make troublesome inquiries about the interest on Annik's hoard. I know too much about Ursule ; she will not meddle, and I shall ask no questions about Lao. Yes ; Lao shall marry Annik. He wants some ready money, and he likes the girl ; and he will take her right away to the west. She will marry him fast enough ; how can she refuse a fine fellow like that ? and I shall be rid of her, and of Monsieur le Curé's visits.   I am tired of being watched over and talked to, as if I were a sick woman."

He stuffed both hands into the pockets of his breeches, which were pear-shaped, and made of unbleached coarse jean gathered into innumerable tiny plaits ; below them came black cloth leggings, trimmed with faded embroidery and buttoned with small metal buttons down to the ankle.

"Annik !" he called, in his hoarse voice—" Annik, I have something to say."   Guérik turned towards the house, but there was no answer.

The road had been empty since Lao departed, but now, here was Annik coming up from the church ; and down the road which Lao had taken came a tall young fellow, walking briskly, whistling as he came. Looking straight before him, a moment ago this bright-haired happy-faced youth had a fearless, honest face which won the beholder ; but as the young girl stepped into the road his fearless look faded into a timid, almost beseeching glance, his well-knit limbs moved less freely, and his head was less saucily erect ; and as Annik saw him, and nodded, and then moved across towards the farm-house, the young man reddened and stopped awkwardly in the middle of the road, as he said "good day."

"You called me, uncle ?" said Annik.

The farmer had turned, and saw the timid greeting exchanged. He answered gruffly,

"Yes—yes. Jeff has need of help ; go, she waits."

A little pout closed the girl's lips. She gave a lingering look over her shoulder, and then went slowly into the house. As she passed her uncle she said dryly—

"Jeff did not need help when I left her. She is growing lazy."

Then she held up her pretty head, and walked on with the air of a young queen.

"I am tired of these airs," the farmer murmured ; "it is not pleasant that a young chit like Annik should be so independent—she shall be tamed. Ah, good day, Silvestik ; you have left work early to-day ; why so ?"

"Yes, I have left work early, Mathurin Guérik. My cousin, the miller of Nizon, is ill ; and he has sent to say that I am to go and help him, that I am to be as his son, and that when he dies, the mill, and all that he has, is to be mine."

"Some folk count chickens through the egg-shell, Silvestik. Well, go your way, and prosper better at Nizon than you have prospered at Kérion. Lao Coätfrec, who went away in disgrace, and who you all said had gone to the bad, has come back to-day rich and prosperous. Go and do likewise."

Silvestik looked sharply at the farmer.

"Lao Coätfrec! has he come back ? Well, I fear his riches are not fairly got ; if, indeed, he is rich. He is a smuggler : every one knows it, and ugly things have happened to him and to his crew."

Guérik's sullen face grew purple, and he growled a fierce oath between his teeth.

"Lao is not a milksop, and so he is a mark for evil tongues. Take my advice, young man," he went on harshly, "keep your mouth shut, or you may find stones in your teeth. Lao is my friend."

Silvestik looked troubled. He had plenty of intelligence, but he was slow in piecing facts together ; and at this moment his head was so full of Annik, that he had no insight into the extent of Guérik's anger.

"I did not know that," he said simply, "or I should have held my tongue ; for I would not willingly grieve you, Mathurin." He stopped and looked sheepish, then he forced out the words, "If all goes as I wish, some day I hope to call you my uncle."

Guérik broke into a coarse, derisive laugh.

"Some folks are bent on seeing through the egg-shell. Go your way, Silvestik. My niece Annik is not for a penniless lad with scarce a beard for the barber. Go, I tell you !"

Guérik roared out the last words. The young man's eyes flashed, and he made a step forward towards the farmer. But Guérik did not notice either look or movement ; as he spoke he turned quickly into the arched doorway, and pushed the half-door violently, so as to prevent any following.

Seeing this, Silvestik paused and unclenched his fists.

"I am as foolish to be provoked by his bluster as he is to show it. He has no power over Annik. If I were richer I would speak to her to-day before I go to Nizon ; as it is, if I were more sure—but she never gives me a smile or a word that she does not give to another. If I thought I had a chance, then indeed——"

He went slowly down the road, past the cottage in front of which Annik had been sitting. Just within, a withered old woman sate with her distaff under her arm, her black cat striving every now and then to touch the ball of yarn as it twirled beside her.

"Good morning, Barba," he said ; "is your rheumatism better ?"

She shook her head. Her white cap fell so low on her wrinkled brown face that scarcely more than the lipless mouth was visible.

"No, my lad ; it is so bad that if I had only legs I would go to Mother Ursule, and ask her to give me a charm for it."

"A charm ! Better ask Monsieur le Curé to pray our Lady to heal you."

The old woman looked up and blinked at him out of her almost shut blue eyes. "I have done that over and over again,—the pain goes, and then it comes back. Mother Ursule's cures are sure, but then it is so far to seek them. Ah ! what it is to be young !"

"Look here, Barba ; to-day I go to Nizon, but to-morrow if I can I come back to Kérion to settle my affairs ; it will not be much out of my way to seek Ursule, and get you a charm against your pain."

The old woman shook her head.

"She will not give it you.   I must seek her myself if the charm is to work.   I would not sit here suffering if another could do my errand, for Ursule never fails. She is powerful: she can change the wind ; she can soften the heart of the proudest maiden and make her say yes.   See my bees ;" she pointed to a range of straw beehives by the side of the cottage.   "Five years ago they would not swarm, but I got a charm from Ursule, and they have always swarmed since.   Ah, she is a wonderful woman."

Here Barba crossed herself, either for protection against the witch, or as an act of faith.

BEEHIVES.

CHAPTER III.

SILVESTIK RESOLVES TO CONSULT THE WITCH.

WHEN Silvestik reached the mill of Nizon he found that his cousin's health had improved.

"I am better; I shall not die directly," the sick man said; "but that makes no difference to you, Silvestik. I shall never walk again, my legs are useless; and you are as much master of the mill as if I lay in the churchyard; but while I live I must keep the name, and I must have a corner of the old house to live in."

Tears rolled down Silvestik's face.

His cousin had always been good to him, but till lately two well-grown sons had barred any hope of succession to the mill. Lately, one of these had been lost at sea, and the other had died of fever—a double grief which had caused the paralysis from which the sick man could not rally.

His young cousin's sympathy cheered the miller, and he agreed to spare Silvestik for a few days, so that he might arrange his affairs at Kérion before he came to settle down for life at Nizon.

That night, when the youth had stowed away his

long legs into one of the cupboard-like bedsteads in the chief room of the mill, he could not sleep. He lay thinking of all that had taken place that day—of Annik, of the farmer's repulse, of the old witch Ursule.

The short-drawn wheezing breath told that the sick man was at last asleep, and for some time past, the grunts and snores of the two servants—the miller's man and his maid—had been sounding through the great dark room. All at once it seemed to Silvestik that he heard the clack of the mill and the plash, plash of falling water, and these sounds joined in a dull chant—"Go to Ursule—Ursule—Ursule," till the words came so close they deafened him—they hurt his ears, and starting awake, he found Jean Marie, his cousin's man, bellowing to him that it was time to rise.

The broad daylight, and the interest he felt in learning his new business, kept Silvestik from thinking of other things, and he laughed and joked all through the morning with the miller's man. When he came in at last from work into the room where his cousin lay, the sick man smiled at him feebly.

"The sight of you does me more good than the doctor," he said. "Who knows, when you are here every day, and I see your fresh face and hear you laugh, and feel, too, that good work is doing—who knows but I may mend and strengthen too ; but that will make no change to you, my lad ; the mill is yours, and the papers will be ready for you to sign when you come back."

He kept on putting off the youth's departure till the light began to fade ; then, as Silvestik bent over the tent bed on which he lay, he laughed, " Bring a wife in thy pocket, young one ; there is enough and to spare for you both, and she will make the place as bright for you as you have made it for me. Do what I say, Silvestik."

" No such luck, cousin." Silvestik turned away hurriedly to hide his red face, and went out through the low doorway.

It is a wild piece of up-and-down road between Nizon and Kérion to travel on a dark night ; moreover, it is bordered on one side by a vast stretch of waste land. On this, sometimes standing up in naked ruggedness, sometimes fallen and overgrown with brown gorse and tufts of heather, are huge mis-shapen blocks of granite.

A hoarse wind had risen after sunset, and had broken up the dull leaden expanse, so gloomy in the daylight, into yet darker but less solid masses, black filmy clouds that drove hurriedly across the sky, as if they actually feared the hoarse voice of the ever-rising wind. It was not late, but darkness had come with a suddenness unknown in England. All at once the howling of the wind lulled, and then a shrieking wail burst over the waste.

Silvestik stood still and crossed himself, and then looked fearfully about. Just in front of him an opening came in the road, and a narrow way went steeply down between two high banks. All around him were the pagan stones, some of which, so tradition said, sheltered dwarfs and korrigans, while some of the taller ones had been known to walk and to crush unwary travellers who met them on their way.

"It was only the wind," he thought, as he stood at the opening of the steep narrow path.

All at once he remembered that it was down such a steep uncanny bit of road as this, only nearer home, that Ursule lived ; and the words of old rheumatic Barba, and his dream of last night, came back—came back so vividly, that it seemed as if a voice from among those dark weird stones were whispering in his ear, " Go to Ursule." Should he go ? Could she teach him how to win Annik ?

He went musing along the high road, difficult to keep to now that waste land spread along each side of the

I

way. Once he went plunging into the midst of this waste among the furze and stones ; and then a cross, placed at the angle of a by-road, caught his eye, and recalled him from his wandering. He took off his hat reverently, and the misty dreams that had been confusing him dispersed for a while.

"Ursule is a witch," he said. "No, I will not seek her, I will speak for myself." But as he drew nearer and nearer to Kérion, his courage failed ; Annik had never said or done anything in the way of personal encouragement. He could not approach her in regular fashion, through the crooked tailor of the village—whose business lay more in the making of marriages than in the making of clothes—for this tailor was a known friend of Guérik's, and would certainly speak to the uncle before speaking to the niece, and thus Silvestik's suit would remain untold.

"If I had only a mother !" the poor fellow sighed. He had been an orphan ever since he could remember ; owing all his teaching to Father Pierre ; and helped on first by one cousin, then by another, but knowing no home except the houses of the farmers with whom he had taken service

Here was Kérion at last. He passed the low cottage where Annik had talked to the cat, and where old Barba had given her counsel, and speeding swiftly up the hill with long, strong strides, he came in sight of the farm-house, a dull red glow through the window beside the door making it visible at some distance. Silvestik stood still and gazed as a lover does gaze on the nest that holds his beloved.   Then his eyes went to the upper story.

"Annik is still below," he thought; "there is no light up-stairs."

Between him and the house, obscuring the red light in the window, came two dark figures, and passed in under the low stone arch of the doorway.   The door was shut-to, and in a minute the dull red brightened, and the window was ablaze with light.   A curse rose to Silvestik's lips; all his pure simple worship of Annik was dimmed by a cloud of furious jealousy.   He had seen Guérik taking Lao Coätfrec to his hearth-stone to woo Annik.

"I was a fool not to guess it yesterday.   I might have spoken then, and so have had her answer before Lao had time to court her with his false words.   He is a thief, and therefore he must be a liar—curse him!"

He plunged his hands into his hair; he stood gazing wildly at the house, while one mad thought and then ar other wrecked all self-control.   Then, with a sudden impulse, he went fast up the hill, on along the road for some distance, till he paused at a cross-road—just such a narrow sunken turning, between two lofty banks, as that where. he had heard the wind shriek over the stone-strewn waste near Nizon.

"I will see Ursule, and ask her help," he said; "right ways are useless against knaves and plotters—they must be met in their own way: who can say how those two may deceive Annik? I must take any means to win her."

But even then his conscience misgave him, and to quiet its pricks he plunged recklessly down the hollow way.

Down, down, it led him, through wet and mire and bramble-tangled paths on to a vast waste. Here it was not so dark as in the narrow way, and the monotonous distant moaning told that the sea was not far off. There was light enough to show pools of water, and in the midst of these was a cluster of huge stones, like a long low hut. At sight of this Silvestik stopped, and his heart beat violently. He tried mechanically to cross himself, but his fingers felt stiff and glued together. A cold dew spread over his forehead, and it seemed to him that the hairs lifted themselves and stood upright on his head. He had never visited this gloomy waste

since he was a child ; but he had been told that the hag
Ursule, shunned and feared by all, lived in a ruined
Dolmen at the end of the narrow road he had descended.
This, then, must be her abode.

Silvestik was brave : he had rescued three men from
drowning at the risk of his own life ; he was an excellent wrestler, and never shrank from any amount of
bodily fatigue or pain ; but he shook with actual fear
at the thought of intruding on Mother Ursule.

CHAPTER IV.

WHAT THE WITCH SAID.

WHILE Silvestik stood undecided and unnerved something touched him, and then, rubbing itself against his
legs, the creature purred. The familiar sound revived
him, and he felt himself again, when a lantern came out
of the group of stones, and a deep voice said.

"Tartare! Tartare! come home ; it is time."

The cat left off rubbing against Silvestik, and moved
towards the lantern : the youth followed the animal,
striving to keep down fear.

"Who art thou ?" He had not nearly reached the
light when this question was sternly asked.

"I am Silvestik Kergroës," he said quickly; "I come to consult you, Mother Ursule."

"Come in, my son, come in "—the voice had a softened, almost a fawning sound in it—" let us see how a poor old woman can help the rich miller of Nizon."

Silvestik started. It was only the day before yesterday that he had learned his cousin's kind intentions; how could the news have already reached Ursule, who rarely went into Kérion?

"I rich! No, no, mother," he laughed, as he followed her, rejoiced to find that she was, after all, an ordinary old woman; "I never expect to be rich."

He followed her through an opening in the dolmen; then he paused and looked round.

Ursule was holding up the lantern, and he saw that he was in a sort of stone vault, surrounded by upright blocks of granite. In the midst was a huge stone table, grooved in the centre, and in one corner, between two lower stones, was a dull smouldering fire. As he looked round to the door by which he had entered, he started violently. In the darkness above the entrance were two yellow eyes glaring at him.

"Come down, Tartare!" Ursule said querulously. "Now, Miller, shall I tell thee what thou hast come to seek?"

Silvestik stared at her in wonder; while the cat sprang down from its post of observation, and nestled on Ursule's shoulder.

She was very witch-like as she stood, the yellow light from the lantern falling on her skinny cheeks and narrow spiteful eyes.   Her face was darker than Nature had made it, from an incrustation of dirt, and tangled grizzled hair fell over it from beneath an old rusty black hood.

"I am not yet the miller of Nizon, mother; my cousin is better and may recover—who knows?'

She shook her fingers in his face, thereby displaying how long-nailed and crooked they were.   Silvestik drew back with a start.   He felt as if those brown claws could hook out his eyes as easily as the yellow-eyed cat on Ursule's shoulder could tear out the heart of a bird.

"'Who knows,'" she laughed.   "You are come, then, to teach, and not to question, young man?"

"I am come for advice, mother; but I have no money to return for it."   He watched her face eagerly, but in the dim light he saw no change from the keen gaze she had kept on him since he entered her den. Then he unbuckled his broad buff leather belt, and threw it on the table between them, the metal clasp ringing on the stone as it fell. "I can offer this," he said timidly.

Ursule laughed.

"What else?" She fingered the belt, pushing out her lower lip contemptuously when she saw how plain the clasp was.

Silvestik looked puzzled. He took off his hat and rubbed his forehead with his orange cotton handkerchief. "I forgot this," he said, and he began to undo the metal buckle that fastened a broad black velvet round the crown of his hat.

"Keep your rubbish, boy, and be speedy," Ursule said fiercely. She flung the belt into one of the dark corners of the den. "Say out at once what you want."

Silvestik's faith in the witch's power was shaken by her contempt of his poverty. How foolish he had been to come empty-handed! and yet, unless he borrowed money of his cousin, he did not know how he could get any sum sufficient to offer to the old witch.

"Come, be quick, loiterer! say what you want," she said hoarsely. She saw that he hesitated, and she was unwilling to lose a fresh dupe.

"I want"—he stammered—"that is, how can a young man who is poor—approach a——"

He stopped.   His downcast eyes and the flush on his honest face told his secret.

" Silvestik Kergroës asks "—Ursule spoke mockingly to the cat on her shoulder—" how he is to win a rich Pennherez,[1] and what steps he is to take to get her for his wife ?"

Silvestik's eyes opened widely, and so did his mouth ; his surprise was unbounded.

" Well, mother," he said simply, " if I had not believed in you before, I believe in you now ; you know wishes before they are spoken."

" He is a young fool, Tartare !"   She had turned her face round to the cat, showing a hideous wrinkled throat in the action.   " He forgets, Tartare, that before a man hints his love he must make sure that a girl will listen with patience, at least."

" Yes, yes, mother, I know she would listen with patience," he said eagerly.   " Annik is sweet and gentle, but I want to know what her answer will be.   Only a hope that she loves could encourage me to ask her, and as she is rich and I am poor "——

" Rich ! ta, ta ! he calls a few hundred francs riches, Tartare.   Annik, indeed ! it is well Silvestik sought our advice.   Annik "—she stood thinking, while the cat nestled its head against her face and purred loudly.

[1] Pennherez is Breton for heiress.

" Boy ! " she turned suddenly to Silvestik—" you have no chance with Annik ; give her up, and choose some one who is less sure of lovers."

" I will not give her up," Silvestik said stoutly ; " if you cannot help me, I will find out by myself whether she will be my wife."

He turned to go, for he was provoked by Ursule's mockery.

She bent forward and caught at his sleeve : her eyes gleamed with anger.

" Listen, fool ! since you will not take a friendly warning ; listen, and be sure you do as I tell you. You shall try the spell. I know Annik ; and if you will succeed with her, you must not give a word or a look of love till you have tried the spell—not even if you see others wooing her.'

" The spell !"—Thoughts of Father Pierre, of the warnings he had often spoken against belief in the pagan traditions that haunt the lands and stones of the country, came back, and made Silvestik hesitate.

Ursule read his face easily.

" Go your ways, fool, and never intrude here again ! I tell you the man who approaches Annik without having first tried whether he can master her love, loses her for ever. Only by the spell can he learn his fate, and if the spell says Yes, it binds her also to be his."

"Well," he said crossly, "what is the spell?"

"Before I tell you, you must swear to do as I bid you—swear on the head of Tartare,"

And she kept her eyes fixed, with a strange constraining power, on Silvestik.

As if the cat understood her mistress's words, it leaped down on to the stone, and sat there, upright and with closed eyes, like a black idol.

Ursule stretched out her lean fingers for Silvestik's hand, and placed it on the cat's head. "Say my words," she whispered. She paused and fixed her eyes on the youth, who repeated her words like a parrot.

"I, Silvestik Kergroës," she said, "swear by the soul of my mother, and by my own salvation "——

At the word "salvation" Silvestik hesitated, but the witch grasped his arm warningly, and he went on—

"That I will, on the night of Saturday, go alone, without telling my purpose to a living soul, to the Rocking-Stone of Tregunc. There I will strive three times to move the stone by gentle pushes of my body and hands. If it remains firm, I may ask Annik with sure hope ; but if it rocks ever so little, her love is not for me : it has been given to more than one before me."

As Silvestik repeated the last words, the cat opened its great yellow eyes, and leaped back to its resting-place on Ursule's shoulder.

Ursule took something from a pocket in her apron, and strewed it on the stone table; then she struck sparks over it with flint and steel. A sudden light flared out and lit up the den with a lurid glare, in which the old woman looked like an animated corpse.

She caught hold of Silvestik's hand, and held it over the flame.

" Swear to do this," she said hoarsely.

" I have sworn already." Silvestik felt sullen and ashamed ; he shivered too, for he believed in the witch, spite of himself.

" But, mother, Pierre Mao did all this," he said, " and a week after his corpse was washed up by the waves on the rocks beyond the Stone of Tregunc."

Ursule did not answer for some moments.

" Silvestik," she said, as the flames died out, and left them in semi-darkness, " that poor fool, Pierre, disobeyed my commands, and so he perished ; if you speak to Annik in the interval, the spell is broken, and the stone will not speak truly, nor can I say what may befall you ; but keep your tongue quiet, and all will be well ; go on Saturday, when the light has faded out of the sky

—go alone, remember : if the stone does not rock, it will hold the maiden's heart fast to yours for ever."

Chapter V.

LAO'S WOOING.

"I wish the good father would come back," thought Annik. "No one else can tell me what to do."

She was sitting at the foot of the tall gray calvary, beside the church, not far from the farm-house ; but the large spreading chestnut boughs in front of this screened her effectually. She hid her face in her hands, though there was no one by to see the warm blood rush up to her face.

She was struggling with a keen dislike to leave Kérion.

This morning, Mathurin had spoken sternly to her. He said he was tired of having her at the farm ; he meant to arrange a marriage for her without delay.

" I do not wish to marry," the girl said angrily ; and then she blushed at her words, and came out to sit under the calvary.

Since the Curé's departure, Lao Coätfrec had come every day to the farm-house, and Annik wondered whether he was the proposed suitor.

"No one shall choose my husband," she said saucily.

Old Barba had often warned Annik that her money was not safe with Mathurin, but when the girl had consulted her only friend, the Curé, he bid her be patient.

"You cannot go out into the world alone, my child, and you do not wish to enter a convent ; you have no relatives, and a home you must have ; be patient, then, and trust in God."

"I wonder what Monsieur le Curé will say now ? I cannot stay here, and yet it would be easier for a *poor* girl to find a home than for me."

Annik sat now with hands disconsolately clasped in her lap.

All at once a shadow came between her and the light : she looked up and saw Lao Coätfrec.

"Good morning, pretty Annik," he said ; and then, without waiting for her answer, he seated himself also on the steps of the calvary.

Annik reddened this time with vexation. If Silvestik or any other Kérion lads spoke to her, they addressed her as Mademoiselle. She thought Lao's manner impertinent.

She looked rather haughty, but the beseeching admiration in his eyes soothed her. "After all," she thought, "the poor fellow can't help liking me.   I need not be cross."

"Did you always live at Auray before you came to Kérion ?" he asked.

"Yes," Annik sighed, "my mother and my aunt and I all lived beside the Loch at Auray.   When my mother died, my aunt married Mathurin Guérik, and we came to Kérion."

"You must find this a poor dull place after Auray," said Lao ; "and a pretty maid like you would take pleasure in a more lively town even than Auray, I fancy. What say you to Brest ?"

Annik looked up quickly ; she was so preoccupied with her own plans for leaving Kérion, that she failed to understand Lao's drift.

"Brest is so far off, and it always seems to me that people must lose their way in a great city."

Lao laughed gaily.

"My dear little country mouse," he said, "Brest could be put in a corner of Paris, or even of Nantes ; but, small as it is, it is full of life ; it is the sailor's home, and you need never lose your way when you have a strong arm ready to protect you."

He looked meaningly into her eyes, and drew close beside her.   But the familiarity of his tone had startled

Annik, and when she met his eyes anger rose quickly in her own.

She looked away, and saw some one coming up from the fountain beyond the church. It was Silvestik, bearing a large water pitcher; behind him hobbled a bent old man, for whom he was carrying it.

Annik nodded to both of them.

"Good day, Jean Marie; good-day, Silvestik," she said; "what news of your cousin?"

She felt sure that this advance on her part would cause the youth to set down his pitcher and enter into talk, thus releasing her from her unwelcome *tête-à-tête*; but, to her surprise, Silvestik only bent his head very slightly, and passed on, leaving her alone with Lao.

She could hardly keep from crying. Ever since it had been said that Silvestik would soon leave Kérion, Annik had felt troubled and restless. He was her favourite among the youths of the village; he was so respectful, yet so anxious to please her; he was good-looking, and, above all, he was liked by the good Curé. But she was very angry with him now; he had looked so sheepish, and it was clownish and ill-mannered to pass on without a word.

The colour rose in her cheeks, and she pouted to herself, "I have been very silly to waste a thought on

Silvestik, he is a foolish fellow." She turned to Lao with a smile.

"I think,"—she spoke as if no interruption had come to their talk, though she was pinching the tips of her fingers to keep down vexation—"I should like to see a great city just for once. I want to see great churches and fine shops; but to *live* in a city, oh, no! I should feel like a bird in a cage."

"No one could ever cage you," he said softly; "you have a spirit, I can see that, and you will always be a free bird; you will always be obeyed."

The flattery of his tone was soothing, but his bold admiring gaze made her eyes droop.

"Women have to obey," said Annik, laughing, and she rose up, thinking she had sat there long enough with Lao.

"Yes, yes, my sweet one; but you would not care to obey a mate like yon poor frightened fool." He pointed after Silvestik. "My faith, a maid will have to ask that lad to wed; he is too much a coward to go a-wooing."

He burst into a loud laugh. Annik reddened and felt guilty; she had known Silvestik much longer than she had known this new acquaintance; why should she join in ridiculing her old friend? And yet she felt sore and angry with Silvestik for his avoidance, and it was soothing to feel that Lao liked to talk to her.

"Well, I must go home. Jeff will be wanting me. Good day, Monsieur Coätfrec ; perhaps some day I may go to Brest."

She nodded gaily.

She looked very charming as she ran away under the spreading chestnut trees. Lao watched her till she disappeared through the round-headed doorway of the farm-house, and then he swore aloud—

" I will have that little girl : she pleases me. But I have learned something sitting here this morning, and watching her tell-tale checks. Guérik is a fool ; he does not see that she can be humoured into anything through her vanity ; but she won't stand driving. She has a temper ; what a rage she got in when that dolt Kergroës passed her by without speaking. I thought the lout cared for her ; I see I was mistaken. Well, I must go and report progress to my grandam ; I have not seen her lately."

CHAPTER VI.

WHAT HAPPENED TO SILVESTIK.

THE stormy night had finally brought a heavy rain-fall, and by Saturday the road leading to Concarneau was a succession of muddy pools. Kérion lay on the waste, some way from the high-road itself; yet, even when this was reached, the deep cart-ruts filled with water looked like continuous miniature canals, and, as evening fell, walking in the obscure light was both difficult and dangerous to the ankles of the wayfarer.

On each side was a dreary moor, covered with heather, so that there was no obstacle to hinder the light and increase the fast-spreading gloom.

Silvestik had left Kérion earlier than he intended, but he hurried along the rough road, reckless of its perils to unwary walkers. He felt despair hanging like lead at his heart. That morning he had again seen Lao talking to Annik, and he thought that the girl looked lovingly at her companion. For a moment Silvestik felt that he must interfere; that he must tell her how unworthy Lao was of her regard; but he remembered the witch's warning; indeed, Annik gave him no chance of speaking; at his approach she turned away.

Now as he stumbled on along the rugged miry road, he asked himself if he was not a fool to go on acting blindly by the advice of Ursule. Only yesterday he had learned the connection between the witch and Lao Coätfrec.

"And yet," he thought, "that could not influence

Ursule's advice. Lao does not want Annik ; he is too bold and free-living to care to be cumbered with a wife ; he is only amusing himself with her."

Ah, if he had only awaited the Curé's return, instead of consulting Ursule, Father Pierre would have told Annik the true character of the man, who was only flattering her, and trying to destroy her peace ; but with the remembrance of the Curé came also a vivid remembrance of warnings he had uttered against pagan superstitions, and specially against the spells used by Ursule.

Silvestik stopped and hung his head with shame. Was he not bound on a godless errand ?   Should he turn back ?

He set his teeth hard.

" No, I cannot lose her. I will try the spell. If the stone remains firm, Annik is mine ; and till Lao came there was a look in her eyes when she talked with me, which at least was liking."

He went on still faster, and just as the light grew very dim he came in sight of the enormous block of granite which goes by the name of the Rocking-Stone of Tregunc.

Silvestik stepped off the road, and went up to the stone. There was still light enough to show that the huge mass rested solely on a projecting angle placed on another block deeply sunk in the earth.

Silvestik looked at the Rocking-Stone, and then he tried to remember the witch's words. He felt a strong reluctance to touch the stone, which in the gloom looked like a dark formless monster; but at the thought of Annik his resolution came back. Placing his hands about midway on the stone, he tried to move it. He might as well have tried to uproot a Menhir. He paused in his effort, and then tried again, but this time, though he set his shoulder to help his hands, the massive block of stone kept firm.

His hopes rose wildly. "She is mine; she is good and true, my sweet Annik; I was a fool to doubt her: to-morrow I will hear from her own lips that she loves me."

He did not feel inclined to make the third trial, when suddenly he heard the purring of a cat. He started, and looked round. The purring came from across the road, and as he looked his hair seemed to lift itself on his forehead. He saw two yellow balls of flame, which he guessed were Tartare's eyes.

He was being watched, then ; who could tell by what evil beings ? and if he failed in obedience he might be torn to pieces.

"And I am in their power, for I have sought their

help." He turned angrily to the stone. This time he only pushed it slightly, and to his dismay he felt it yield under his fingers, and, as they still touched it, it continued to rock for some seconds.

Silvestik gave a wild cry of despair, and rushed on across the road, heedless how he went, in the direction of Tartare's eyes. He felt a stunning blow, and then he fell senseless beside a huge mass of granite.

Chapter VII

WHAT ANNIK HEARD IN HER BEDROOM.

ANNIK had been unhappy all day. She had slighted Silvestik, and she had allowed Lao to speak to her too freely, and this evening he had come in to see Guérik, and had again spoken familiarly to her, as if there were an understanding between them. And when she looked scornful and angry, the farmer patted Lao's shoulder and encouraged him to go on.

" It is the way with women, friend Coätfrec," he said, winking at him ; "they always say No when they mean Yes."

At this Annik flamed into indignant words, and running up the staircase ladder to her little room, she drew the bolt across the door, resolved not to go down till Lao had taken his departure.

She sat half-an-hour in the darkness thinking of Silvestik, and puzzling over his strange behaviour. From below came the sound of men's voices, broken by the flapping of the chestnut leaves against her window. She began to feel tired of waiting. Lao was still talking to her uncle. She had no candle, and through the wide chinks in the rough flooring of her room the red fire-light peeped in lines here and there.

"I am tired," Annik thought, "I shall not go down again to-night," and she began to prepare for bed.

The large silver-headed pin which fastened her bodice slipped from her fingers and fell on the floor, and she stooped hurriedly, lest it should roll through one of the crevices. She felt for it in the darkness, and as she found it, a flush of joy glowed on her cheeks. Silvestik had given it her as a fairing last year when she had danced with him at the Pardon of Pont-Aven. But the glow faded quickly into a trembling chill of fear, and instead of rising from her knees, Annik lay down on the boards, placing her ear on one of the larger crevices marked by the line of red light that glowed up from the room beneath. She had heard her name spoken by Lao, coupled with the word "wife."

"Trust me," Guérik said in answer, "Annik shall be your wife in a week."

"Why not sooner? I can ill spare a week; my mates will be getting unruly, and I should have liked a day or so with the little one in Brest before I go off again. Why cannot I wed Annik on Monday?"

Guérik laughed. "You are a fine fellow to lecture me about dealing gently by the girl, and then to want to marry her out of hand without any approaches."

"Leave me alone, my friend; I know the sex." Lao's laugh made the girl shiver as she lay listening. "I told you that three days ago. Meantime Annik and I have not kept apart; and"—the speaker paused, as if he looked round to secure himself against a listener; he went on in a lower voice—"I have learned something else. Mark you, this is between ourselves—that young fool Kergröes, with all his sheepishness, is mad with love for Annik. He has sold his soul to my grandmother for a spell to charm the girl's love."

"And are you fool enough to believe such old women's tales, Lao? I should have thought even Silvestik had more sense. What may this spell be?"

Trembling in every limb, Annik lay straining her ear to catch the answer.

"Ursule has sent him to-night to the Rocking-Stone.

She tells me the spell will fail, but that its power will drive Silvestik distracted, and that probably he will rush on to the sea, and be carried off by the waves, as that poor fool Pierre was carried some years ago, for Ursule has fixed the time for trying the spell at the turn of the tide. This must not come to Annik's ears. A woman, however pretty, is such a fool, that if she hears of a man running a risk for love of her, she loves him at once, and, who can say, perhaps gives herself up to his memory. Silvestik will not be missed for a week or so ; folks will think he is at Nizon. It is a good plan—aha ! my grandmother is a clever woman."

Annik lay as if spell-bound ; her senses seemed to be going ; but just then a bough struck the window, and she roused.

"There is yet another question." Annik's heart throbbed so painfully that she could scarcely bear to listen, and yet she must hear all—she feared to lose a syllable of her uncle's answer. " Suppose Silvestik comes back safe and sound ?" There was a sneer in Guérik's voice.

Lao swore a frightful oath, and the girl heard him rise violently from his seat and stamp on the clay floor.

" He will not ; he is too great a fool. Ursule swore to him that if the spell failed, he had no chance with

Annik, and weak lads such as he is have no courage to persevere.   He will never come back to Kérion."

"Do not you be too sure of that, Lao Coätfrec; while there is life there is hope. For an hour or so the lad may give way to despair, but after that he will say to himself that he cannot make matters worse by speaking to Annik, and he may make them better; and, to tell you the truth, I fancy the foolish girl likes him. Yes, yes, if the tide does not carry him off, my friend, he will come back and try his chance."

"Then"—Lao spoke coolly, but in a determined voice—"he must not come back to Kérion."

There was silence after this.   Presently Guérik spoke and Lao answered, but in such low voices, that Annik could not distinguish words.   It seemed to her, from the dull continued murmur, that the two men were carrying on the talk in whispers.

Annik rose up softly from the floor. She felt strangely calm and alert. One thought ruled her—to leave the house as quickly and silently as she could, and to warn Silvestik of coming danger.

She dared not go down-stairs; she could not open the heavy house door, which she had heard her uncle close, without risk of noise; she dared not even undraw the bolt of her room. But she saw her way of escape clearly, and at once set to work to reach it.

Her room was but half the size of that below, half being boarded off and used as a receptacle for fodder. There was a square opening in this boarded partition, with a bit of canvas nailed across to screen off the draught which came through a window opening in the hay-loft.

Annik cautiously dressed herself, and then, with a pair of scissors, she cut open the canvas screen that divided her from the hay-loft. Once more she listened, but the dull murmur of voices had not ceased.

There was more light from the outer opening in the loft than had come through Annik's window, though a chestnut tree stood close to the house on this side also, but the nearest branch had been scathed by lightning, and was now leafless.

With her shoes in her hand, Annik got through the opening from her room into the loft. Slowly and softly, step by step, feeling her way as she went on, she groped across the hay and bean stalks till she reached the outer opening.

She leant forward and stretched out her hand till it touched the long scathed branch that reached across the back of the house—it was no new experience for Annik to descend by the chestnut tree. Often when her uncle's rude words had made her run upstairs in anger, she had got out of the house by this means, and now she soon found her way to the branch and from thence quickly to the soft ground below, for the rain had made mire of the yard behind the house.

She paused and listened. She could only hear the movement of the cows within the house; she slipped on her shoes, and started off in the darkness towards Tregunc.

CHAPTER VIII.

WHAT ANNIK SAW AT THE ROCKING-STONE.

HEAVY-FOOTED, for the mud clung in lumps to her shoes, tired, yet too overwrought to be sensible of fatigue, Annik at last reached the road beside which stood the Rocking-Stone, and before long the vast mysterious mass loomed in the darkness.

She looked round her. The dull sound of lapping waves told that the sea was not far off, and southwards the lightness of the horizon pointed out its whereabouts.

The dull sadness of the sound recalled Lao's ominous words—"He must not come back to Kérion."

"Silvestik! Silvestik!" she cried, in an agony of terror, "where art thou? It is Annik who calls."

From across the road came a voice she knew well—the voice of the good Curé.

"Who goes there? If you are a Christian man or woman, in the name of God come and help a dying man!"

A thrill of terror passed through Annik.

"I come, I come!" she cried.

And she went in the direction of the voice, slipping and stumbling over the uneven ground ; and soon, in the darkness, she saw the priest bending over some one who lay outstretched at his feet.

Without a word she flung herself down beside the senseless body, and chafed the cold hands, till at last she fancied they moved within her own.

The Curé spoke, and she answered, but it seemed to Annik that she was some one else, and that she heard her own voice speaking to the good father, " Beware of Lao and of Guérik," she said, "they will murder Silvestik."

Presently came footsteps, and a light beamed up the road. Annik rose to her feet, and she saw her uncle and Lao.

She stretched out her arms and spoke vehemently—"Keep off, cowards and murderers ! You shall not touch Silvestik."

But as she spoke she grew faint and giddy ; and as Lao answered her soothingly, she sank on the ground.

"Mathurin Guérik," the Curé said sternly, "go back at once for your horse and cart to carry these children home. As to you," he said to Lao, "begone—you are not wanted."

This was all Annik heard, and then she knew no more.

Annik opened her eyes, and wondered as she looked round her.

"Aha!" a cheery voice said from the chair beside the bed, "you have slept late, my poor Annik; you must rise now, for Monsieur le Curé wants a talk with you."

Jeanneton, the Curé's old housekeeper, patted the girl's cheek, and handed her a cup of coffee. But Annik could not drink. She sat up gazing in the cheery old face with eager straining eyes. She feared to ask the question that hung on her lips. The old woman seemed to understand the questioning look.

"Silvestik is all right," she said. "It is well to be young," she went on, and she shook her head reproachfully. "Monsieur le Curé permits much to young people, or I would ask what you and Silvestik Kergroës had been about when the good father found you and brought you both home half dead last night."

"And he?"—cried Annik, with a burst of sobs.

"He!" Jeanneton shrugged her shoulders. "He is in the parlour with Monsieur. But he is a fright, I can tell you, with his bandaged head and broken arm—poor fellow! You seem to have come off best, mademoiselle," she added crossly.

But Annik flung her arms round the old woman's neck, laughing, and crying, and sobbing all at once, in a most incoherent manner—a manner which, as Jeanneton afterwards told her master, was quite unsuited to a presbytery.

But for all that, Annik stayed on at the Curé's house till the chestnut leaves grew brown, and began to fall slowly from their stalks, and then, one fine clear morning, Silvestik and Annik were wedded in the little village church of Kérion, and went home to Nizon to live at the mill.

Lao Coätfrec never came back to Kérion, though Mathurin Guérik still lived on in the old farm-house; but Annik never crossed its threshold after her marriage.

CHAPTER VI.

OUR next halt after Quimperlé was at the little town of
Auray, 'which is among the most pleasant of Breton
towns, quaint and quiet, sleeping beside the river of
the same name.

It possesses no public buildings worthy of remark;
and though in the oldest quarter there still remain many
picturesque houses dating from mediæval times, the
charm of the place consists chiefly in its pleasant position beside the river, almost surrounded by wooded
hills. It is pleasant of an evening to see the women
sitting in front of the quaint old houses, knitting or
spinning, while their tongues go as fast as the whirr of
the wheels.

Within a drive are to be found the stones of Carnac;
and a day will take the traveller to the remarkable
scenery and antiquities of Loc-maria-ker and back.

A few miles from the town is the church of St. Anne
d'Auray, celebrated for its yearly pilgrimages. Many

THE BRIDGE, AURAY.

thousands of pilgrims flock thither from all parts of Brittany ; and the scenes both inside and outside the

OLD WOMAN SPINNING.

church are most picturesque and entertaining. Among other curious ceremonies, the pilgrims go up and down the steps of the Scala Santa on their knees. There is

L

also a miraculous fountain, and countless bowls and vessels full of the healing water are drunk there. Blind and lame beggars drive a "roaring trade" at this spot.

Close to Auray is the establishment of the Chartreuse; it occupies the site of the chapel that the Duke of Brittany, John the Fourth, caused to be built upon the field of the battle of Auray. Near the church belonging to the convent is the famous Champ des Martyrs; and here, too, stands the monument to the memory of the emigrés and royalists who fell at Quiberon, or were shot on the banks of the Auray.

All these places of interest make the little town of Auray a very desirable place to spend some days in In the woods round Auray wolves used to be plentiful; and probably the scene of the Lai of Marie de France was not far from Auray.

The Bisclaveret.

A BRETON LEGEND ADAPTED FROM THE LAI OF MARIE DE FRANCE.

ONCE upon a time there lived in Brittany a noble gentleman of great worth and remarkable beauty. He was in high favour with his prince, and was dearly loved and honoured by his friends. To crown all, he had lately married a lovely lady of high degree, and she loved him very tenderly. They were as happy as the birds in springtime; but after a while one circumstance troubled the young wife's happiness, and caused her many hours of sad and anxious thought. She observed that regularly every week her lord went away from home for three days. She asked him the reason, but he either made no reply or else evaded her inquiries. Then she questioned some of the old retainers, but no one seemed to know what became of their lord during the three days of his absence from home.

Time passed on, and she grew yet more troubled and suspicious.

One day her lord came home in a more joyous and affectionate humour than was usual to him, and the lady thought this was the opportunity she had been seeking.

She returned his caresses very tenderly, and then entreated him to explain to her the mystery of these frequent absences from his castle.

"But for them," she cried, "I should be truly happy; surely you will remove this cloud from my mind.

The lord looked sorely troubled, and he turned his face from her with a deep sigh.

"You must not question me, my beloved," he answered ; "it may be that if you do, you will altogether destroy our happiness."

But her curiosity was far stronger than her love was, and at last, overcome by her fond importunities, he confessed his fatal secret. He told her that he was a Loup-garou, or a Bisclaveret, as the Bretons call the creature, and that during the three days of his weekly absence from home he roamed the forest hard by in the form of a wolf.

> " Dame jeo deviens Bisclaveret,
>   En cele grant forest me met."

The lady's heart grew cold with horror ; but she hid her surprise and dread as well as she could, and continued her questions—

" Do you roam this forest in your clothes ?" she asked.

" No," he answered, sadly.

" Tell me then," she said, coaxingly, " what you do with your clothes ?"

But her lord shook his head and withdrew himself from her arms.

" I may not satisfy you on this point," he said, " for if by any chance I were to lose my clothes, or if I were even seen in the act of taking them off, I should be condemned to remain a loup-garou until my clothes were restored to me."

The lady burst into tears.

" Ah, how unkind you are," she sobbed, " Mon Dieu ! what have I done to forfeit your confidence. Tell me, my husband, what risk can there be in trusting your secret to your faithful wife ?"

Under the influence of these words, and the like, and many caresses, the poor gentleman once more yielded.

" You know," he said, " the ancient ruined chapel near to where the four roads meet in the forest. There I find at these times safe shelter. In a thicket near there is a hollow stone, under which I hide my clothes."

The lady said nothing ; but she thought much. She was greatly disturbed by all she had heard ; she was married to a loup-garou ! and this was anything but a pleasant fact to ponder on. She shuddered whenever she looked at her husband, and the result of her meditations was, that she determined to get rid of him. But she kept her plans to herself, and dissembled like a woman who knows all the tricks of her sex. She affected even more than her usual love for her handsome lord.

There lived in the neighbourhood another cavalier, who was passionately in love with the wife of the loup-garou. Up to this time she had treated him with great coldness—but now he came into her mind ; he was not so handsome as her lord, but he was not a loup-garou. She changed her behaviour towards him. During the absence of her husband she sent the cavalier an invitation to come and see her, giving him to understand that she was willing to accept his love and his service. The cavalier, full of joy, hastened to present himself before her. Their interview was long and satisfactory ; the lady told him of the secret trouble that had come into her life, and demanded his aid to release her from it ; she told him at the same time what had passed between her husband and herself about the concealment of the clothes—and what would befall if they were taken away.

"Do you think that any union is binding to such a monster as a loup-garou ?"

" No, by heavens !" said the cavalier, who then expressed the most devoted love for her, and pledged himself to do all she wished. So they parted.

From that day the unfortunate husband was no more seen ; his friends and his relations sought for him in vain. His wife also made a show of great grief at his strange disappearance, and caused diligent search to be made, but before many months had elapsed she married the cavalier.

Just at this time it happened that the king had passed a whole year without hunting, and all at once he felt violently inclined for a day's sport in the forest.

Now the forest in which the king was accustomed to hunt happened to be the very one in which our poor Bisclaveret had been condemned to wander. The king summoned his noblest attendants, and set out for the chase. Almost as soon as the hounds were uncoupled, they discovered the poor animal, and dashed after him as he fled at their approach. They pursued him all through the day; already he had received several wounds, his strength was almost exhausted. The hounds were closing in upon him, and he was preparing for the last struggle, when he perceived the king; in an instant he darted up to the prince, raised himself against his stirrup, licked the prince's leg and foot, and, by his pitiful moans and almost human look, seemed to implore his protection.

At first the king was alarmed by this strange incident, but finding no harm come of it, he quickly recovered himself. " Hold off," he said to his followers, " and call off the dogs ; I forbid that any injury should be done to the poor animal which has sought my protection." To his astonishment the creature seemed to understand him. It at once became quiet, and stood beside his stirrup, looking up at him with grateful eyes. The king was more and more surprised ; he at once gave orders to return to the palace. He said he had had enough sport for that day. The wolf followed close behind the king, like a dog, and when they reached the palace went up with him even to his chamber. The courtiers tried to interfere, but the king, yielding to some strange influence, bade them let the beast alone.

So it came to pass that the wolf was in great favour both with the king and the whole court.

He spent his days among the courtiers, who delighted in his intelligence and his gentleness, but every night he slept at the foot of the king's bed.

Not very long after the capture of the loup-garou, the king determined to hold a cour plénière, and to give greater importance to the occasion he invited all his barons and vassals to be present. The cavalier who had married the wife of the loup-garou came among the others. As usual the wolf was at his post close beside the king. But when the cavalier advanced from the crowd to pay homage to his prince, the wolf uttered a wild cry, sprang upon him, threw him down, and bit him very severely.

There was a loud clamour, and all was confusion, but the king shouted to the animal, and it immediately slunk back to its place beside the royal chair. Every one was astonished at this sudden outbreak of fury from so tame and gentle a creature, which had hitherto behaved more like a lamb than a wolf. But many who witnessed the attack shook their heads, and said it was very strange ; there was more in it than they could understand.

The cavalier was furious ; he would have killed the wolf if he had not feared the king's displeasure. However, he promised himself an early day of vengeance.

Some time after this the king went again to hunt in the forest where he had met with our wolf. The creature went with him ; it seemed as though it felt that there was no security for it away from the king, and, indeed, the king himself, moved by his affection and by some strange sympathy, had commanded that the animal should be always with him.

The faithless wife of the loup-garou, hearing of the royal visit to her neighbourhood, requested an audience. Her request was granted, but as soon as she entered the king's presence the wolf sprang at her, as he had sprung at her husband, and bit off her nose. Swords were quickly drawn, and the woman was rescued from the furious animal, which would have been most certainly cut to pieces, but a wise man among those present took the creature's part, and begged his assailants to hold their hands a while, "there is something strange in all this ;" he said, "I counsel His Majesty to imprison this lady till she confesses, if she is able, what cause for hatred this wolf has against herself and her husband."

At first the terrified woman denied all knowledge of this beast, but after a while—faint and suffering, and seeing that her imprisonment was resolved on—she told the story of the loup-garou, and confessed her sin against him. She said that she and her present husband had stolen his clothes from under the stone where they were hidden ; and then bursting into tears, she said, "And this wolf is doubtless my former lord."

The king then demanded if any of her lord's clothes were yet in her possession ; and when she answered "Yes," he bade her send and fetch them instantly. This was done, and the clothes were placed before the Bisclaveret, but he seemed to take no notice of them. Then the wise man who had before spoken said it was probable the loup-garou would not put on his clothes or undergo his metamorphosis in public.

The king agreed with this opinion, and he himself took the loup-garou into his own bedroom, where he left him alone with the clothes.

Some hours after he returned accompanied by two of his barons—and to his wonder and delight he saw his long lost favourite asleep upon the royal bed.

At this sight the king could not restrain his joy ; with a loud cry he ran to him.

The noble wakened at the noise, and sprang to his

feet rubbing his eyes. The king threw his arms round him, and kissed him on both cheeks, crying out how happy he was to see him once more.

He immediately restored to him all his former honours and possessions, and also bestowed many rich gifts upon him. The faithless wife, and the cavalier who had helped her to accomplish her treason, were ignominiously banished the kingdom. The guilty pair lived some years after, and had several children, and strangely enough the girls were all born without noses.

CHAPTER VII.

From Auray the drive to Vannes is very pleasant, though at first sight Vannes seems dull and wanting in colour in comparison with the picturesque towns of Finistère. But it is the capital of Morbihan, and within reach of it are some of the grandest and weirdest of the monolithic remains that make Brittany so specially interesting. As we stayed on in Vannes, and found out its quaint twisted streets and charming fragments of old wall built up between houses, its Tour du Connétable, with the washing-place in the river below so full of light and shade, its evening walks in the tree-shaded Garenne, we grew warmly attached to the old city so full of historical memories, and were loth to leave it. One of its best local antiquaries, Mr. Alfred Fouquet, had died not long before we reached Vannes. He not only made some very useful researches in Carnac and elsewhere, and published a most useful little manual for the use of travellers in search of the real wonders of Brittany, but he had begun to collect real legends from the lips of the peasantry, and had published a book, now, alas! out of print, containing a collection of these. We tried vainly to get a sight of this book, but even his widow did not seem to possess a copy of it ; however, we heard one or two of the stories, and the following is said to be in M. Fouquet's collection :--

The Glover of Vannes.

THERE lived in Vannes a great many years ago an honest and devout glover. His nearest friend was a tailor who lived in the place Henri Quatre, but he lay a-dying, and his friend the glover had stayed with him till a late hour doing all for him that he could.

Late as it was he saw, as he passed the cathedral that the doors were still open, and he turned into the church and knelt before the altar of one of the side chapels.

There was scarcely any light, almost all the worshippers had departed, the place was wrapped in deep silence, and the poor glover, exhausted by his grief and by many nights of watching beside his sick friend, soon began to nod.

He roused himself, but he soon fell off to sleep again, such sound sleep that neither the jingle of the keys nor the sound of the locks, nor even the angelus bell, roused him awake.

All at once the clock struck twelve, and then the glover started and rubbed his eyes; he was stiff with cold, and he could not remember where he was. It was no longer dark, and as he opened his eyes wide awake now, he saw standing before the altar at which he knelt a priest garbed in a black chasuble embroidered with a large white cross. The altar was draped in black, and two wax candles stood on it; by their pale light he saw on each candle a death's head and crossbones.

The glover was much surprised and deeply impressed by what seemed to him a funereal scene, but as he was always more ready to help others than to think of himself, he soon remarked that there was no assistant present, and he went and knelt down before the priest to act as server.

As he knelt down he glanced at the priest's face—

Oh, horror! the priest was a skeleton with hollow eye-sockets and fleshless cheeks.

The terrified glover fell senseless on the ground, and there he remained till the morning angelus bell roused him, and he went home to his family.

From this time he was a changed man. All the serene gaiety that had once characterised him disappeared, he became morose and silent even towards his wife, and he scarcely noticed his children. Above all things he dreaded sleep ; it no sooner visited him than he was filled with fear, horrible dreams and frightful nightmare soon banished sleep, and made bedtime a penance to which he looked forward with dread.

At last, afraid that his reason was deserting him, he resolved to confide all to his spiritual guide, and he implored the good priest to shed, if possible, some peace into his soul.

"My son," said the priest, "you are in error ; why should you thus fret and disturb your soul about that which is perhaps only a delusion, but which, if it is real, should be made a matter of serious inquiry ? Either Satan tempted you during that night in the cathedral, or you are chosen by God himself to expiate some negligence or sacrilege committed against him. There is but one way, my son, if you would regain peace here on earth and assure your eternal salvation : you must watch in the same place and at the same hour for the return of the visitation which has so shaken your nerves."

"Oh, my father," cried the glover, "do not lay such a penance on me. The terror of it will infallibly destroy me."

"If you go to the chapel trusting in your own

strength," said the confessor " you will doubtless perish ; but, my son, you well know that faith is our sure shield, and that prayer is a most powerful weapon. Pray and believe, and if the spectre reappears, question it boldly in the name of the living God ; bid it tell you in whose name it comes. Go, my son, I absolve you, and may God be with you."

That very evening—strong in faith, but weak in spirit—the glover went to the cathedral. He knelt before the altar in the same chapel, but he did not fall asleep ; he heard the gates and doors lock, but he did not think he prayed fervently till the dreaded hour came.

The first stroke of midnight sounded, and all at once the two candles on the altar lit of themselves. The altar was draped in black, and the skeleton priest in his black chasuble appeared on the threshold of the chapel.

" Hold," cried the glover, " if you come in the name of Satan I charge you to depart from this holy place ; but if you come in the name of Almighty God, speak, and tell your need."

" Listen and believe, my son," said the spectre in a stifled voice ; " for years, oh ! such long years of suffering, I am doomed to wait every night at this altar till some good Christian comes to serve at a mass which I pro-

RUE DE JERZUAL, DINAN.

mised to say, and which I first neglected, and then forgot. This fatal neglect and forgetfulness have closed heaven, not only against me, but against the soul for which the mass should have been said. Blessed art thou my son whom God has chosen to save two souls."

He ceased and knelt down before the altar; the glover knelt beside him, and the mass of the dead was said; but as the priest uttered the words "depart in peace," he disappeared; and the glover looking up, saw through the window two broad rays of light going up heavenward.

The glover wiped his forehead, and then waited till the angelus bell sounded; then he returned to his family with his wonted happy smile, for his mind had recovered its balance, and peace reigned in his soul.

CHAPTER VIII.

WE found the scenery of the valley of the Rance most
charming and romantic ; on the side and summit of a
rocky steep in this valley the town of Dinan is built,
and its effect from the river is exquisitely picturesque.
The town itself is very interesting ; the older quarters
abound in quaint houses, with overhanging stones and
arcades on granite or wooden pillars.

The Rue de Jerzual, the subject of the illustration,
is of great length ; it leads down almost to the water's
edge, and presents a succession of quaint old houses,
forming many charming pictures. This street is so
steep, that it is a labour to climb ; it was originally the
only approach to the town on the St. Malo side. Now
the splendid granite viaduct which spans the valley
(begun in 1846) enables one to avoid this laborious
ascent. The piers of this viaduct rise one hundred and
thirty feet from the bed of the river.

The castle, built early in the fourteenth century, with its machicolated donjon, is very picturesque; it is a fine and well-preserved specimen of military architecture. Anne of Brittany lived in it. Bertrand du Guesclin withstood a siege in this castle, the public place of Dinan was the scene of the famous combat between du Guesclin and the English knight, Sir Thomas of Canterbury, in 1359.

It was during the siege of Dinan by the Duke of Lancaster, that this duel *à l'outrance* took place. The account of it is taken from a life of Du Guesclin by Émile de Bonnechose. Bertrand du Guesclin was in Dinan with his young brother Oliver; a suspension of arms for forty days having been signed, Oliver, relying on the treaty, went out of the town without any misgivings, and approached the English camp. He met on his way a very strong and valiant English knight, by name Sir Thomas of Canterbury, who stopped him, seized his person, and taking him by force to the camp, kept him prisoner in his tent. When the news reached Bertrand, he grew red with fury ("S'y rougit comme charbon "), says the old chronicler, and having learned the name of the false knight who held his brother captive, cried out, "By St. Yves, he shall soon give him up." Bertrand immediately mounts his horse, gallops to the English camp, and arriving at the Prince's tent, demands an audience. He enters and finds the Duke of Lancaster playing chess with the celebrated Sir John Chandos, surrounded by the principal barons, among whom are Robert Knolles and young Montfort.

The prince having recognised him, said, "You are welcome, Bertrand." And as Bertrand bent the knee before him, Lancaster left his game, held out his hand to him, and raised him up. The English barons also welcomed him, and Chandos offered him wine ; but Bertrand answered that he would not lift a glass to his lips until justice had been done him for the foul outrage offered to his brother. He then told them how his brother Oliver had been taken captive, contrary to all right, by Canterbury, and demanded that he should be delivered up to him at once. Lancaster immediately summoned the accused to his presence and ordered him to answer the accusation. Canterbury, trusting in his strength, and full of wrath and arrogance, answered that if Bertrand du Guesclin imputed to him an action unworthy of a knight, he must prove it by sustaining his cause in person sword in hand, and so saying he threw down his glove.

Du Guesclin rushed to pick it up. "False knight," said he, "perjured and traitor, I will prove it on thy body ! I will fight thee before all the barons. I swear by the true God that I will not sleep in a bed nor break bread until I have had the right of thee in full armour at the point of the sword."

Lancaster gave his consent to the combat, and Chandos presented Bertrand with a horse as a mark of his esteem.

When the inhabitants of Dinan heard of this duel of Du Guesclin in enclosed lists with one of the best champions of England, they were moved with lively fear for him whom they considered their strongest defender. All of them great and small offered prayers to God for him.

Then a noble young lady, by name Typhaine Raguenel, renowned for her beauty and wisdom, calmed their apprehensions. She was the daughter of one of the richest inhabitants of the town, and had so high a reputation for learning in astrology and other occult sciences, that she was considered a witch by the common people. "Do not be alarmed, good people," she said to the townsfolks of Dinan ; "fear nothing for Bertrand, he will be the victor in this conflict." These words were repeated to Du Guesclin ; but he was then far from foreseeing the close ties which should hereafter bind him to this noble lady, and he said, "You should not pay heed to the vain words of a woman, I put all my confidence in God and in my right."

It was decided that the combat should take place in the large market-place of Dinan, in the presence of the Duke of Lancaster ; that the town should give hostages, and that the Prince should be admitted with a train of a hundred knights and barons chosen by himself.

As the day approached, Canterbury began to lose courage, and Robert Knolles, in his name, attempted to make an accommodation with Du Guesclin ; but Bertrand was too much incensed ; " If he does not wish to fight, let him give himself up to my mercy, and present me with his sword, holding it in his hand by the point."

" He will not do that," said Robert Knolles. " He is right," said Bertrand, " honour is worth more than life."

The lists were duly opened in the great market-place of the town, under the presidentship of the Duke of Lancaster, surrounded by his knights, and in the presence of the governor of the city, the Sire de Penhoen, and a vast assemblage of the inhabitants.

The two champions appeared, armed from head to foot, and their horses also completely covered with steel.

The signal given, they urged their horses forward with fury, and threw themselves, sword in hand, one on the other. The combat was long, as they seemed of equal strength. The blows they gave each other were terrible ; the swords struck fire from their armour, but it was impenetrable, and no blood flowed. At last they seized hold of each other, each attempting to drag the other from his horse.

In this struggle the Englishman dropped his sword, whereupon Bertrand quickly sprang down into the arena, seized the sword, and threw it over the lists among the crowd. Canterbury now had no weapon but his dagger or poignard ; but he was on horseback while his adversary was on foot, and driving his horse against Du Guesclin, he prevented his remounting, and pursued him across the arena, hoping to crush him under his horse's feet.

Du Guesclin avoided him with difficulty, as he was impeded by his armour. At last he sat down to unfasten his knee-pieces, and then, as the Englishman threw himself again upon him, he sprang adroitly to one side, plunging his sword, as his enemy passed, into his horse's side. The animal bounded with the pain, reared up, and threw his rider. Du Guesclin darted forward, seized the Englishman by the throat, and pressing his knee on his chest, struck him several blows on the face.

The Duke of Lancaster at this juncture interfered, the knights ran forward and called upon Bertrand to spare the vanquished.

"Grant his life to the Duke," said Robert Knolles; it is enough, all the honour is yours. "I grant his life to the Duke," said Bertrand; and advancing towards the prince, "Sire," he said with respect, "if it had not been for obedience to you, I would have killed him."

"He will not fare much better," said Lancaster; "you have fought valiantly. Your brother will be restored to you, and I will give him a thousand livres to equip himself. The arms and horse of this felon knight are yours; I do not love traitors, and he will come no more to my court."

Lancaster and his followers returned to the camp. Oliver was restored to his brother and the day ended with a grand fête given by the inhabitants of Dinan to the conqueror, and at which was present the beautiful Typhaine Raguenel, who had foretold the victory.

She went by the name of Typhaine la Fée, from her reputed skill in magic and her astronomic studies. She was rich as well as learned; and in 1360 Du Guesclin asked her in marriage. The wedding was solemnised at Pontorson, which Du Guesclin at that time governed in the name of the King of France.

Typhaine seems to have been a very fit wife for a hero, and the marriage was a very happy one.

The heart of this valiant Breton knight was buried

RUINS OF THE ABBEY, LÉHON.

beside his wife, the Lady Typhaine, in the church of the Jacobins at Dinan, but now church and heart and tomb have disappeared. A black stone in the cathedral gives the lying intelligence that Du Guesclin's heart reposes there, while his body is at St. Denis ; the hero's house is in the Rue de la Croix. Dinan is still surrounded by strong walls and massive watch-towers, and the old gateways also remain.

The general aspect of Dinan and the country around are alike charming.

> " De ce splendide paysage
> Qui nous retracera l'image ?—
> Venez bardes mélodieux,
> De cette tribune de pierre,
> Voir le ciel sourire à la terre
> Voir la terre sourire aux cieux."

Within an easy walk is the village of Lehon, one of the pleasantest and prettiest of Breton villages. Once it was famous for a castle and an abbey, now both in ruins. The castle of Lehon was one of the most powerful in Brittany,—built on the top of a steep hill overlooking the village,—but little of it now remains. The ruins of the abbey are far more perfect, and, as the illustration shows, form a very picturesque feature in the landscape, as they stand embosomed in trees beside the sunny smiling Rance, that prettiest of Breton rivers

—so pretty that it perhaps loses some of the character-istics of Brittany—the weird pathos of its stone-covered landes and the turbulence of its rocky brawling streams.

CHURCH, LEHON.

The Story of La Garaye.

THE poem, "The Lady of La Garaye," had inspired us with a very ardent wish to see the ruins of this famous chateau — famous in so remarkable a way —not for sieges sustained and heroic feats of valour, but for succour and solace given to hundreds of poor suffering human beings by its skilful and beneficent lord and lady ; for the local record of the story of the Count and Countess of La Garaye speaks of Count Claude as the prime mover in this great work of mercy, of which his lady's accident suggested the idea.

We went out of quaint picturesque old-world Dinan by the old gateway along the shaded Boulevard, under the walls of the exquisitely placed town, which looks down on all sides on charming and wooded country.

Soon we came into a pleasant green valley, with a distant view of grand old trees. This valley led us into a sort of rocky pass, where trees met overhead, a most refreshing resting-place on this hot August after-noon. Soon after we came in sight of the grand old avenue of beech-trees. These were exquisite in colour, light, and shade, as the level sunshine poured its brilliant flood over the grassed drive, while the massive boles of the trees cast broad bands of shadow across the golden floor.

THE CHATEAU OF LA GARAYE.

There is a loneliness even in the beauty of this old avenue — reaching to a length of more than two hundred yards—so silent now that we found it difficult to

realise that human habitation was near, and this feeling
of loneliness and desolation deepened to intense melancholy as we drew near the actual entrance of the
château.

The crumbling gate-piers of La Garaye are covered
with ivy, and trees have sprung from their tops.   The
entrance-court is cumbered with blocks of ruined
masonry——some completely mantled with ivy, others
bright with fern ; over all thorny red-stemmed brambles
flaunt their long arms boldly, as if asserting possession.

The château is a complete ruin, except the well-
known, almost perfect, bit that stands in the vegetable
garden.   This bit is exquisite in colour, yet more beautiful, perhaps, in its decay than when it was whole.

It seems a harsh mockery to gaze at this lonely
bit of ruin from the well-stocked fruit garden of the
farmer who now owns La Garaye, and makes market
out of the pilgrims who visit the site where so much
good has been practised.   It is a disgrace to the
country that Monsieur de la Garaye's noble work
should not have been revived—for the hospital buildings still remain ; an effort at least might be made to
prevent the total destruction of his fair home.   For
month by month stones fall from La Garaye, the bats
and owls that haunt the clustering ivy, as they swoop

to and fro in their night revels, shake and loosen clinging fragments, and send them into the bosom of the wild
picturesque luxuriance below, a tangle of nettles and
brambles extending all around, starred here and there
with golden-eyed blossoms, while tufts of flowering
grass and faithful snap-dragon still haunt the walls of this
pathetic ruin, and seem to kiss the mouldering stones.

It is difficult at first sight to picture La Garaye as
it was in the first married years of Count Claude, and
in the first part of that eighteenth century which
changed the destinies of France, and branded her fair
bosom with ineffaceable scars.

Claude Toussaint Marot, Count of La Garaye,
baron of Blaizon, Viscount of Beaufort and of Taden,
and lord of many other places, commander and grand
hospitaller of our Lady of Mount Carmel, was the
richest and most powerful noble of his time near Dinan
when, on the death of his eldest brother, he succeeded
to the family estates. He was as gifted and as handsome as he was rich and powerful, and he was univers-
ally beloved. He had married a lovely and loveable
lady,—Marie Marguerite de la Motte-Picquet,—the
heroine of Lady Stirling-Maxwell's exquisite poem ;
but, as has been said, one hears less in local traditions
of the Lady of La Garaye than of her husband, though

it was doubtless the blight thrown on her early married life that roused this devoted pair from their frivolous course of gaiety and self-pleasing.

Though the Château la Garaye is only a heap of ruins, there are still fragments enough left to show that it was a richly adorned building of the sixteenth century. It must have been a splendid abode, filled, as it was, with every then known luxury, and crowded with honoured guests who helped the gay, pleasure-loving pair to waste their days. Banquets and balls, shooting and hunting, and all the other amusements of the period, were to be found in perfection at La Garaye; and the hunting train of richly dressed guests and followers, splendid horses and dogs, is said to have been a grand sight to witness as it issued from the castle gates, and caracoled under the splendid beech trees. The Countess La Garaye, specially famed for her grace and beauty of movement, was passionately fond of hunting, and a most accomplished horsewoman, and she delighted in sharing every pursuit of her beloved lord. One day while following the hounds with her husband, she was flung violently from her horse; she was carried home insensible, and supposed to be mortally injured. Her life was, however, spared, and Mrs. Norton tells this part of the story most touchingly:

how when sense returns to the sweet Lady of La Garaye
she hears the " grave physician's" fiat that she will be

" Crooked and sick for ever."

> " Long on his face her wistful gaze she kept,
>   Then dropped her head and wildly moaned and wept,
>   Shivering through every limb, as lightning thought
>   Smote her with all the endless ruin wrought.
>   Never to be a mother !   Never give
>   Another life beyond her own to live,
>   Never to see her husband bless their child,
>   Thinking (dear blessed thought) like him it smiled :
>   Never again with Claud to walk or ride,
>   Partake his pleasures with a playful pride,
>   But cease from all companionship so shared,
>   And only have the hours his pity spared.
>   .   .   .   .
>   And she repeated with a moaning cry,
>   ' Better to die, O God !—'Twere best to die.' "

She had lost all beauty, and the grace of movement
for which she had been so famed could no longer be
exercised.   She was now a sickly, crippled woman,
sighing and sobbing life away.   Her husband gave up
many of his out-door pursuits to sit beside her sick-
bed, but all in vain ; it seemed to her that she was de-
priving him of the joys in which she could no longer
share, and that soon he would find the time thus spent
beside her an irksome burden on his pleasures.   Try
as he would, he could not reconcile the beloved sufferer

to submit to the blow which had so suddenly crushed her existence and left her hanging like a broken lily on its stalk, between life and death.

The death of a dearly-loved brother who was visiting them at Château la Garaye threw a yet deeper gloom over their saddened life. The Countess could not well be more grief-stricken and despairing than she already was, but to Count Claude this fresh blow was overwhelming. His brother's death had left him indeed alone.

He went to gaze for the last time on the face of this beloved friend, and his anguish grew beyond all control. The silence of the priest who knelt beside the dead man irritated the Count almost to frenzy. "Ah, father," he exclaimed, "how happy you are; you are free from all the shackles of earthly love; you do not know the meaning of suffering."

The priest rose from his knees and looked tenderly at the mourner. "You mistake, my son," he said gently; "I love all who suffer, but I submit to God's will, and I bend myself resignedly to the blows he deals me, whatever they may be, because they are dealt by Him."

Monsieur de la Garaye was greatly struck. Was there then, he asked himself, less misery in submitting to than in murmuring against God's will?

Some time after this, tradition says that Claude de la Garaye had a vision ; he dreamed that he came home one winter's night late from a long day's hunting. The ground beneath the beech-trees of the great avenue was covered with snow, and the bare branches rattled in the keen north wind. All at once the Count saw advancing towards him a white horseman surrounded with flames, flames too seemed to hover round his white steed. Claude reined up his horse and waited till the apparition came closer to him.

"Claude de la Garaye," it said, "if you really wish for happiness, you must change your whole life. Give up your frivolous pleasures, and spend your abundant riches in relieving the poor and afflicted, so shall the blessing of God be yours in this world and in the next. I, your brother, who died so short a time ago in your arms, am sent to give you this warning."

Claude la Garaye waked from his dream and pondered his brother's words, and during that night he is said to have made the resolution which changed the whole course of his life. He told his wife of the warning he had received—she was now to a certain extent convalescent,—and, in spite of her weakness, she resolved to go with him to Paris, there to gain the scientific knowledge necessary for the project they had both determined to carry out at La Garaye.

For three years the Count carefully devoted his whole time to the practical study of medicine, surgery, and chemistry, and made rapid progress therein, while his weak and crippled wife studied ophthalmic surgery at the Hotel Dieu. So skilful did she become that she was ultimately most successful in performing operations for the removal of cataract at the Hospital of La Garaye.

The noble pair began their studies in the year 1710, when the Count de la Garaye was thirty-six, and at the close of their three years' noviciate they returned to La Garaye, and laid the foundations of the large range of buildings which still exists on the western side of the Château. They gathered round them a skilful band of doctors, surgeons, and medical students, and were soon able to open their hospital to the poor and suffering, whom they tended themselves most devotedly.

The fame of the hospital spread ; patients flocked to it from all parts of France. Louis XV. was so touched by the generosity of the La Garayes, that he sent for the Count and invested him with the Cross of the order of St. Lazare, and gave him 75,000 livres.

It is said that Monsieur de la Garaye would rise and attend his patients at any hour of the night. His ordinary rule was to rise at half-past four in summer, in winter a little later, and study in his laboratory till seven, then to join with his patients in family prayer ; after this he dressed the wounds of his poor people, went to hear mass, and then breakfasted. After breakfast he tried scientific experiments, visited the hospital at eleven, presided at the dinner of his patients, and when they had dined he took a frugal meal himself.

After dinner he talked to his workpeople and labourers, or went out shooting. At four o'clock he came home and saw his patients. Eight o'clock was supper-time, with religious reading. At half-past nine every one went to bed, except those who tended the sick.

On Sundays and festivals the Count himself preached to his guests, as he called the poor sufferers he watched over.

The Countess seems to have been not only a ministering angel among the patients whom she nursed devotedly by night as well as by day, but also a saviour of many souls whom she brought back to the faith and ordinances of their youth. The noble pair were deservedly loved and reverenced by their patients and throughout the country round.

The Hospital of La Garaye was not the Count's only good work. During one very severe winter he not only sold a great portion of his plate to relieve the general distress, but he employed a great number of poor people whom the terrible famine that then ravaged France had brought to ruin in reclaiming and cultivating vast wastes belonging to his estates. He also founded at Dinan the Hospital for Incurables which still exists, and at Tardu a Convent for Charity School-girls.

' In 1720 Marseilles was desolated by the plague,—hundreds of people died daily. When the tidings came to the ears of Monsieur de La Garaye he at once offered his personal services to the Archbishop. But his crowning act of self-devotion, and that which should make the name of Claude de la Garaye for ever dear to Englishmen, happened during the war between France and Great Britain in 1747. He had been ready enough to take arms, and to arm his tenants and dependants, at the first hint of foreign invasion ; but when he heard that two or three thousand English prisoners were shut up in the Castle of Dinan, and that the prison was so overcrowded, and the captives so neglected, that a malignant fever had broken out, Monsieur La Garaye did not shrink from the danger, although the fever had destroyed not only many of the unhappy English, but the doctors and nuns who tended them.   He came at once to Dinan, and by his skill and timely succour saved many lives.   The English seem to have been much impressed by his benevolence.   One nobleman presented him with six thorough-bred dogs, and Queen Anne (the French biographer must mean Queen Caroline) sent him two others, each wearing a silver collar.

The Count of La Garaye went on with his work till he was eighty years old, and then died sitting in his arm-chair—died peacefully as he had lived, without apparent suffering.   He and his wife both lie buried in the little graveyard at Tardu, their graves being marked by very simple tombs against the wall of the village church.   The Count's has this inscription :—

Cy gitte corps,
de Messire Claude Toussaints Marot,
Chevalier, Comte de la Garaye,
Décédé le 2 Juillet, en son chateau,
1755.

CHAPTER IX.

DOL—A LEGEND OF ST. CHRISTOPHER—THE OLD WOMAN'S COW —THE HOME OF CHATEAUBRIAND—CHÂTEAU COMBOURG— VITRÉ.

IF for no other cause, the town of Dol must always dwell pleasantly in the minds of the authors of this book in connection with a certain huge fig-tree in the garden of its Inn of Notre Dame. The weather was hot, and the ripe excellent fruit most refreshing ; and at going away the kind landlady presented us with a dainty basketful packed in glorious leaves, the contents of which proved most grateful on the journey.

But Dol is a quaint and interesting town, and has a very fine cathedral, older and in purer style than most Breton churches ; and besides it has a special attraction to the traveller about to enter Normandy. From the summit of Mont Dol, a little way out of the town, can be seen through a glass the famous Mont S. Michel.

Dol seems to form a connecting link between Normandy and Brittany. The bridge, with its groups of ancient houses, is a very picturesque object ; the water below is generally gay with knots of quaintly capped women—for the caps of Dol are some of the most remarkable in Brittany—washing brilliant bunches of carrots and turnips in the swiftly flowing water.

OLD HOUSES, DOL.

The legend of St. Christopher goes back to the days before this bridge was built.

A Legend of St. Christopher.

"Christopher the strong-shouldered" was in great request as a ferryman, and at the time I write of he kept the ford of the river, and carried many burdens over it.

One fine day, the legend says, our Blessed Lord arrived at the ford with his twelve apostles. Christopher took first our Lord and then each of his followers, one after another, in his gigantic arms, and carried them across to the farther bank of the river.

Our Lord bade Christopher name his reward.

St. Peter came up and whispered softly in his ear, "Ask for Paradise, and you will be happy."

"Mind your own business," said Christopher in a surly tone ; then to our Lord he said reverently, "As you offer me a gift, O Lord, I ask that whatsoever I wish for may come into my sack."

Our Lord consented ; but he told Christopher never to wish for money, or for anything he did not really need.

Time went on. Christopher kept to his bargain, and the sack was only filled with bread, fruit, and vegetables, and, be it said in justice to the ferryman, it was frequently emptied to give to the poor. But after a while Christopher fell into temptation.

It happened one day that as he was passing along the main street of Dol, he stopped before the shop of a money-changer, where piles of gold and silver coin were arranged in little heaps.

Now Christopher sinned in gazing at the money,

for it is a step towards covetousness to gaze on that which we are forbidden. Eve, you know, looked at the apple before she touched it. The Evil One was close at hand, and he began to whisper in Christopher's ear, " See here, my fine fellow, think how much good you may do to others with all this gold and silver ; why, you can build houses for the poor, and clothe them and feed them besides ; think of that, my friend. Now you have only to wish, and the money is yours."

The idea was too tempting to resist ; Christopher wished, and lo ! there was the money in his sack. You must remember that, though he was good, he was only a man after all, he was not even a saint in those days.

As might have been expected, this first yielding to temptation was followed by other yieldings, and though he was liberal he did not spend on the poor all the money that had come into his sack.

One day he had eaten a luxurious dinner, and had lain down on the grass to rest in the shade.

Presently who should pass by but the Evil One, who began to mock and gibe at Christopher.

The giant was not of a patient disposition, and before long he and the mocking fiend were fighting out their dispute ; their strength was so fairly matched that the battle lasted two days without any chance of a victory on either side. The thick grass was worn away, and the ground dinted by the pressure of their feet, and the blows they dealt one another sounded like repeated hammer-strokes, and were heard from afar.

They might indeed be fighting still if a lucky thought had not come to Christopher.

"Ah, cursed one!" he exclaimed, "in the name of the most Holy, get into my sack."

No sooner said than behold the Evil One is in the sack, and Christopher, tying the string round its mouth, throws it over his shoulders.

But now what shall he do with the prisoner?

Going along the road he comes to a smithy where a blacksmith and two brawny assistants are beating out red-hot iron.

"Happy thought," says Christopher to himself; to the blacksmith he says—

"See here, neighbour, I carry a dangerous beast in this sack, he has done all sorts of mischief; if you will undertake to hammer him as thin as a penny piece, I will give you a crown."

"A bargain," cries the blacksmith, and he and Christopher clasp palms upon it.

The blacksmith and his men hoist the sack on to

the anvil, and, spite of the howls and contortions of its inmate, they hammer at him all through the night.

At length, when day begins to break, a feeble voice comes from the sack.

"Christopher, Christopher, I give in, I am beaten; on what terms will you let me out?"

"You must swear to obey me whenever I require you to do so, and leave me in peace for evermore

"I swear," says the feeble voice.

"Depart," says Christopher, "and may I never more behold thee."

From this time Christopher's whole life changed. He gave himself up to good works, and when his strength failed him, so that he could no longer perform his duty at the ford, he took refuge in a little cell, on the ruins of which were built a church dedicated to St. Christopher. He lived many years in his cell, given up to prayer and penance, his saintly reputation causing the hermitage to be the resort of numerous pilgrims.

Notwithstanding all this, when, after his death, St. Christopher presented himself at the gates of Paradise, St. Peter, remembering how his advice had been slighted, refused Christopher admittance.

The poor saint went sadly away, hanging his head,

and, not taking any heed where he trod, he went by mistake down the broad steps of hell.

He went down and down a great many steps, and came at last to a door kept by a pleasant-looking youth.

"Come in, I pray you," said the youth.

Christopher was stepping across the threshold when his old adversary, who stood just within, perceived him.

"No, no!" he cried, "we will have none of him. I know who he is ; turn him out ; he is more than a match for me."

So poor Christopher was forced to go up again, and once more he found himself at the gates of Paradise. Strains of lovely music came from within, and the saint sought more than ever to enter and be with the blessed.

He went close up to the gates. "My Lord Peter," he said, "what wondrous music you have inside your gates—I pray you of your charity to leave them ajar, so that a poor outsider may enjoy these exquisite sounds."

Saint Peter's tender heart was touched, he opened the gate a few inches. Christopher dexterously flings his sack inside the gates, and, following it, he seats himself thereon.

"I am on my own ground now," he says; "you cannot turn me out."

And Saint Christopher has stayed in heaven ever since. Surely his repentance has earned him a good place there.

The following is another quaint legend of Dol :—

The Old Woman's Cow.

ONCE upon a time St. Peter and St. John were taking a journey through Brittany. They visited every house they came near, rich as well as poor ; they preached in the churches and chapels of the towns they passed through, and sometimes they preached in the market-place in the presence of all the townsfolk.

One spring day they climbed a long and steep hill. The sun was hot, and they were thirsty, and there was not a drop of water to be seen. St. Peter was the most sanguine nature of the two. "We shall find a house on the top of the hill," he said.

When they reached the top they saw a farm-house sheltered among some trees.

"Let us go in and ask for some water here," said Saint Peter, and in they went.

A little old woman sat beside the hearthstone, and not far off a little child lay sucking a goat.

"Grandmother," said St. Peter, "will you be so kind as to give us a little water?"

"Yes, surely, good gentlemen," she answered readily. "I have plenty of water, good water too, but I have nothing else in the world."

She filled a bowl with water from her pitcher and gave it to the saints to drink.

They drank eagerly, and then they looked at the sucking infant.

"That is not your child, grandmother," said St. Peter.

"No, surely not, but I love him as though he were my own. My daughter died in giving him birth, and I have to take care of him."

"Has he a father?"

"Oh yes, he has a father who goes out to work every day at a gentleman's house not far off; he gets his food and eight sous a day, and that is all we have to live on. When my husband was alive things were different; he was a farmer, and we had cows and pigs, but all are gone now."

"Suppose you had a cow now," said St. Peter.

"Ah! indeed, good gentleman, suppose we had, we should be happy enough. Though we have no longer any land I could take the cow out and let it feed along the roads, and we should have milk and butter to sell on market day.   But what is the use of supposing ; I shall never have a cow again."

"Never you mind, grandmother, lend me your stick a minute," said St. Peter.   .

St. Peter took the old woman's stick and struck a blow on the broad hearthstone, and behold, there was a beautiful strawberry cow with udders full of milk.

"Holy Virgin !" exclaimed the old woman, "however did that cow get here ?"

"By the grace of God, grandmother ; it is for you."

"May the blessing of God rest on you, good gentlemen.   I will pray for you night and day."

"God be with you," said the saints ; and they went on their way, leaving the old woman lost in wonder as she gazed at her cow.

The cow gently lowed.

"What a fine creature !" she said, "and how full she is of milk.   I must milk her.   But where can she have come from ?   Just from hitting a stick on the hearth-stone ; nothing can be easier than that.   Well, here is my stick, and there's the hearth-stone.   Ah, if I had only just such another cow !   I wonder if I could bring one by just hitting my stick on the stone."

No sooner said than done, and behold out sprang an enormous wolf, which fastened on the cow and killed her.

Out ran the old woman—she hurried as fast as her legs would carry her after the two saints.

"Gentlemen! gentlemen!" she cried, quite out of breath. As the saints had walked slowly on account of the heat they had not got very far; they heard her calling and waited till she came up.

"Whatever has happened, grandmother?" said St. Peter.

"Alas, gentlemen, my cow, my cow! You had hardly left me when in came a huge wolf and sprang upon my beautiful strawberry cow."

"But what had you done first, good mother?" said St. John very gently.

"I—I hit my stick on the hearth-stone," said the old woman, hanging her head.

"The wolf came because you summoned it," said St. Peter gravely. "Go back to your house, and you will find your cow safe and sound. But, grandmother, be wiser in future, and be content with what God sends you."

Back went the old woman to her house, and found her cow safe and well, lowing softly for she wanted to be milked; and then the dame understood that God's saints had visited her.

O

Château Combourg.

A VERY short railway journey from Dol brought us to the small but picturesque town of Combourg. It has an old-world aspect, as the greater part of the houses are of the sixteenth century.

But the most interesting building there is the castle, in which Chateaubriand, the famous author, spent some of his boyhood—the castle still belongs to his family—and his chamber is preserved in the state it was in when he lived at Combourg. It is in one of the towers, and hither has been brought the simple furniture which was in his room at Paris during the latter part of his life. A small iron bedstead, an ordinary wooden table, an iron inkstand, an iron crucifix, and an iron holy water stoup. Chateaubriand gives a too highly-coloured picture of his home in his *Memoires*. He calls it an immense castle, which would accommodate with ease 100 knights and their attendants; a third of this number would be more like the truth.

The castle, dating from the fifteenth century, is a square building flanked by four large machicolated towers ; that at the north-east angle is higher than the

CHATEAU COMBOURG.

others (Chateaubriand called it "tour de Maure"), and it appears to belong to the fourteenth century.

The castle, with its many towers, with their conical roofs rising above the surrounding trees and ancient houses, is very picturesque. Château Combourg suggested to the poet the lines beginning—

> " Combien j'ai douce souvenance
> Du joli lieu de ma naissance."

Chateaubriand was really born in St. Malo, Rue des Juifs, in the house which is now the Hotel de France. From the window of the room the tomb of the illustrious author can be seen standing alone on the islet called Grand Bey. It was his own desire to be buried in that lonely spot. The position of the tomb, on the rocky verge of the islet overlooking the vast expanse of ocean, is very impressive.

We were sorry to reach Vitré, for it was the last interesting town in Brittany, and we felt that our holiday was over. It is a wonderfully old-world town. Modern improvements, which will doubtless soon set in in a flood, are only beginning there. Its castle, its feudal ramparts flanked by towers, its old houses which seem to totter on their supporting pillars—have a truly mediæval air. There is something inexpressibly pathetic about its aspect—pathetic and grotesque also, for it looks full of strange stories—moss and lichen thrive on its roofs and stonework; it seems to be perpetually moaning over its past.   Though it is nearer

OLD SHOPS, VITRÉ

France than the utterly French city of Rennes, Vitré is a true type of an old Breton town.   Its streets are narrow and twisting, and up and down, and badly paved also; the houses are some of wood, with often quaintly carved beams, and some of stone; in many of them the upper story projects considerably, and is supported on oaken pillars covered with slate. The Rue Poterie is the quaintest and strangest of these streets. Here one can go back to the middle ages; one fancies even that the open shops, shown in the illustration, are scarcely changed from what they were in the sixteenth century, or in the days of Madame de Sévigné. The chief inn in the town is called Hotel de Sévigné, and here you see a suite of rooms which Madame de Sévigné is said to have occupied; on the tiles of the flooring are various crests, which it seems she had a fancy for collecting. In one of these rooms is a secret sliding panel, with a recess behind it; here one fancies she may have kept secret papers, or the letters of Pauline.

The castle is equally picturesque and interesting. It was founded about the end of the eleventh century, and rebuilt in the fourteenth and fifteenth; the walls are covered with slate. Standing on a hill it commands the surrounding country, and must have been a strong fortress. The initals of Guyonne, Countess of Laval and Marquise de Nesle, occur frequently here, in the monogram, G. L. N., on the entablature of the charming little tourelle which she built here in 1560; on each side are shields bearing the arms of France and of Laval, with the motto, " Post tenebras spero lucem." She was a Huguenot, and the inscription " is supposed to be in allusion to the darkness of the old religion as compared with the faith of the Reformers."

There is a very quaintly sculptured stone pulpit outside the church of Notre Dame ; on this grotesque figures of demons express, by face and gesture, great dislike to the doctrines preached above them.

Les Rochers, the charming country-house from which so many of Madame de Sévigné's letters are dated, is within an easy drive of Vitré. Madame de Sévigné's bedroom has been left untouched, there is her bed of red and white silk falling to pieces with age, and there is the escritoire on which her delightful letters were written,— her account-books still lie on it. Outside the drawing-room windows is a long range of orange trees in tubs, and two of these are said to have been planted by Madame de Sévigné herself.

CHAPTER X.

AVRANCHES—A BRACE OF CHARACTERS—THE STORY OF THE "PILGRIMAGE TO THE MOUNT."

WE had been spending some delightful weeks in Normandy, beginning at Etretat, and then journeying along the sea-board, with its groups of watering-places, so dear in August to tired Parisians, till we reached quiet primitive Arromanches. We made a pleasant halt in this newly built village, with its old world inhabitants —its magnificent sun-flowers making a foreground with their immense bronze disks, to the masts and rigging of the fishing-boats drawn up high and dry on the beach, and the belt of blue sea beyond ; but we could not linger long ; we were impatient to reach the real bourne of our journey—the wonderful Mont St. Michel. So on we went from Bayeux, through lofty St. Lo, Coutances, with its grand cathedral and charming gardens, beautiful, dirty, and unsavoury Granville, till we found ourselves at last at pretty, bright, sunshiny Avranches, so exquisite in its position and surroundings and the view it commands, and yet in itself so tame and uninteresting.

We found the sparkling clean little place full of bustle ; all the inns were crammed, and when we made inquiry we learned that this concourse of visitors had been caused by the pilgrimage.

"What pilgrimage ? " we asked our voluble femme-de-chambre, who, having once been a beauty, expected a good deal of notice still from those she waited on.

"Comment !" she exclaimed. "is it possible that Madame does not know of the great pilgrimage to Mont S. Michel—pilgrims come to it from all parts ; what do I know—from Jersey, Guernsey also—from England perhaps," she added, " if," with a sly look, " there are any good Catholics in Madame's country."

We asked how long the pilgrimage would last.

"Oh, that depends ; three or four days if all the pilgrims arrive in that time, but to-morrow is the grand day ; ah, that will be a sight to see ; the Bishop of Coutances himself will say a mass, and he will perform the benediction service in the crypt of the Gros Piliers : Madame knows that the black Virgin is there, and that is why it is called the Chapel of Notre Dame-sous-terre. Ah !" she put both hands suddenly to her ears, and then extending her arms shook her fingers, "do but hear the bells, Madame. Ah, Mon Dieu ! I must run, if Madame will have the goodness to excuse me."

This news put us into a pleasant state of excitement ; we should have preferred to see the Mount in its weird lonely grandeur, still there was something very fitting in the idea of a pilgrimage to Mont S. Michel, and we determined to go there to-morrow.

We went to order a carriage in the town, but the driver was out, and we were left in doubt, for it seemed that every vehicle and every horse in Avranches was going on pilgrimage next day.

We came in and dined at our comfortable, but not too liberal, table d'hôte, and then mounted to the bed-room at the tip-top of the house, which our friend Rosalie, the coquettish and communicative femme-de-chambre, told us we were very lucky to get.

We had hardly seated ourselves when a knock came at the door, and a strange man's voice inquired if Monsieur and Madame les Anglais lived here.

This was our driver, a little crooked fellow with a most comical face ; he seemed to be laughing at himself; he began by asking just half as much again as he meant to take, but we shook our heads ; he then grumbled extremely at having to carry two people with one horse, while we assured him we could not think of paying the price he asked for two.

At last he stood still and scratched his head for

some seconds without speaking—then he shrugged his shoulders and exhibited the palms of both hands.

"So be it," he said ; "I will take Monsieur's price. The pilgrimage is like everything else—it is not what it was at first—why, the last pilgrimage to Mont St. Michel, ah, Mon Dieu !"—up went his shoulders again —"that, if you please, was something like. At Pontorson, there were not beds enough to lie on; the pilgrims slept in sheds—on pavements—anywhere. I drove a cart full of pilgrims across the sands; ah, yes! I remember there was a story told of one of them next day, poor soul."

"Can you tell us the story ?"

He shrugged his shoulders at our eagerness, and shook his head.

"I knew it, bah !"—he began to think, screwing up his little eyes, and making his comic face so absurd that we could scarcely keep serious.

"I knew it," he repeated—then he slapped his leg joyfully. "Ma foi, my wife knows every word of it,— she never forgets a story,—and if Madame likes I will go home and listen, and then to-morrow I shall be able to tell it as glibly as any old chatterer in the country."

And next day he certainly whiled away part of the long drive from Avranches by telling us the story of the " Pilgrimage to the Mount."

A Pilgrimage to the Mount.

PART I.

MOTHER AND SON.

IT is Michaelmas, and the streets of a gray old cathedral city in France are busy with the tread of feet and the buzz of voices as the inhabitants take their way to High Mass—some to the cathedral and some to the numerous old churches of the town. Overhead the weather is fine; there are only a few snowy wool-like clouds, but these are so bright, and they keep their places so firmly on the blue vault above, that there is no fear of rain. A crisp wind scatters the dust briskly along the Boulevards, and whirls the yellow leaves off as if the year were a month older. There is a sighing movement, too, every now and then, among these trees, which seems to tell that the leaves are conscious that the best part of their life is spent, that old age, with feeble heart-beats and sapless limbs, is near, and death treading on its heels.

The Boulevard will be full enough this afternoon, but no one stays there now. Every one is going to Mass, though it is yet early; but to get a seat in the cathedral one must be early to-day, for Monseigneur the Archbishop is going to preach ; so the little square outside the splendid hoary building is full of townspeople.

PORCH OF CATHEDRAL, CHARTRES.

The small houses which face the cathedral are very near it—so near it that they are always in a cool grey shadow. The door of one of the smallest of these houses stands open, and shows inside a dark narrow passage, with a black door on one side, and a staircase beyond. A small slender woman stands at the foot of the staircase ; she has a young slight figure, and she is dressed with much simplicity and neatness. Just now her snowy capped head is thrown back on her shoulders, as she stands calling to some one overhead :

"Eustache, my child, come quickly, or you will be too late."

"I come, my mother," is answered in such a sweet silver treble that it takes one by surprise,—a surprise which anticipates the sweet boyish face of the golden-haired child who comes carefully downstairs, not taking half a flight at a jump, as would seem better suited to his age, but with an enforced quietude that does not belong to his bright eyes and expressive features. He holds up one slight finger at his mother, and makes a slight sound with his mouth ; then he takes her hand and draws her quietly to the entrance door. She has so sweet a face, but yet she is not like her child, not even when she smiles down into his dark eyes. His face is square both at brow and chin, and one feels by instinct that though those dark eyes may always be sweet in expression, yet there is a promise of intellect in them which will make him yet more unlike his mother ; for hers is a flower-like face, a delicate skin with a tinge of pink colour, yet touched with the soft melancholy of a Madonna—oval in its outline, with small and regular, not insignificant, features, and eyes of the palest blue; these eyes glisten, and the glow blooms brightly on her cheeks as she listens to her boy.

He speaks eagerly now that he has reached the outside door.

"Never fear, little mother,"—he pats her hand fondly between both his own; "I shall be as punctual as the rest. I said 'Hush just now because of Julie;—but indeed she is better to-day; and when I told her I had warmed the soup myself, she said it was twice as good, and now she is sleepy, mother; and when I pat her shoulder softly, she shuts her eyes and opens her mouth,—yes, yes"—he screws up his own rosy mouth importantly—"Julie will sleep and she will get well. Allons, I must go to church:" then stopping suddenly, he looks up with a grave face: "Mother," he says, "how enormous is the mouth of Julie!"

A little later his mother watches him as he walks in procession, the fairest of the choir children, his lovely treble notes ringing through the lofty aisles of the cathedral. He does not see her as she kneels behind one of the massive piers, and gazes with tenderest love on his rapt face while he sings.

How fervently she prays for her Eustache,—he has elected to become a doctor ; for, child as he is, he so loves to tend the sick, and his mother prays that the studies he will have to follow if he adopts this vocation may not harden his heart.   She prays, too,—and all unconsciously tears stream over her sweet face— that he may never lose his love and reverence for holy things and holy places, a love which she has taught him by word and deed.   " Oh my God," she prays, " spare me such bitter pain as this."

For to Marie Texier's simplicity it seems that the worst trial she could be called on to suffer would be to see her Eustache's love and faith grow cold.

" If he forgot to worship, it would be worse than losing Jean Baptiste over again," she thinks.   Jean Baptiste was the tenderly-loved husband of her youth, who died when Eustache was but five years old, so she prays with all her strength for this dearly-loved child.

But service is over now, and she hurries home to get his meal ready for Eustache.

She has quite a little feast for him to-day.   Soup and some mussels, pieds de cochon and radishes, daintily arranged on a fine white tablecloth.

Eustache soon comes out of church, and flies across the street, his dark eyes glowing with delight.

He kisses his mother, and then says grace reverently, and sits down and eats his soup in hungry silence, but when he gets to his second mussel he pauses, and looks anxiously across the table.

"Mother, what do you think?   Father Cléry has said that my voice is a good one."

Madame Texier smiles.

"Yes, yes, my child ; your voice is true and sweet, but," she adds humbly, "I am thankful that the good father should think so."

Eustache gives his mother a long yearning look, and then he goes on eating his mussels.

His young mind is burdened with a new idea, and it is too large a one for him to carry alone.   He would share it with Madame le Camac upstairs if it were less important, but it seems to him a kind of treason against his sweet mother to confide it to other ears than hers.   And yet, young as he is, he knows something of the love his mother has for him, and he feels that this new idea will somehow prove distasteful to her ; but he knows and feels these things dimly, he has only instinct to guide him, poor little bright-haired Eustache.

But his mother is watching him ; her love is too all-absorbing not to be alive to the slightest change in her darling. Eustache is not a chattering child, but he is always full of life, and especially on a holiday; he has always a plan for the happiest way of spending it.

Marie Texier watches him as he goes on eating in silence, and as he draws his thick dark eyebrows together and looks down in his plate, she grows more and more sure that something troubles her darling.

She is too reserved and timid to ask him at once what ails him; the question would come more easily if Eustache were near her, and she could put her arm round him and draw his fair head close to hers; but the table is between them, and the boy does not look at her.

All at once he lifts his head. He has not noticed his mother's unusual silence, he has been far too deeply occupied with his own reverie.

"Mother," he says abruptly, "Is your heart set on making me a doctor?" He gives a sigh of relief at this beginning.

Marie Texier's soft eyes open with surprise.

"It is not I," she says gently, "who chose that state of life for you—you said you should like it, my child—if you wish for a quieter life perhaps a post may be found for you in the library."

Madame Texier's husband had been one of the

public librarians, and to her this was the best of all employments.

Eustache shakes his head, he is a little vexed with his mother, it seems to him that she ought to be able to guess his wishes.

At last he bursts out abruptly.

"Father Cléry says my voice is a great gift, and he says a gift should be for God's service."

Madame Texier looks puzzled.

"Your voice is good now, my child; but who knows. Voices change, and sometimes never come back. Do you mean that Father Cléry wishes you, when you are old enough, to become one of the singers of the cathedral? Well, then, you may be a singer, and you may earn your living some other way too, my darling."

Eustache shakes his head.

'No, no, little mother, I would not be one of the singers if I could, they—they are not good; they are dirty, rough, and noisy; but never mind them little mother; Father Cléry means something else."

Marie Texier gives a little start; she understands now, and she turns so pale, that if Eustache were less intent on his idea he would think she was ill. As it is, he feels dimly that what he has to say must give her pain, and he gets off his chair and comes and stands beside her.

"Well, little mother," he says rather impatiently, "you do not ask any questions?"

"I am listening," and she puts her hand softly to her heart as if she felt some pain there.

But Eustache has got too eager to notice anything.

"Father Cléry says," he speaks very earnestly, "that we should give our lives up to God's service; and he said just now, 'You can give a great gift to Him, Eustache;' and I said, 'What, Father?' and he said, 'You can give your voice;' and then he said,—listen little mother;" for Marie covers her white face with one trembling hand. "'You should go to the seminary, Eustache, and when you are made a priest, you can come back here again and be close to your mother,' so you see, darling mother, you could listen to me every day."

But Marie does not hear the last words; she feels a sudden spasm of pain, and then she falls back so white and rigid that Eustache is terrified out of his self-absorption.

"Julie," he cries in terror, "Julie, come quickly,"—but no one comes; and while he stands panic-stricken gazing at the blanched face and lifeless attitude, he remembers that Julie le Camac lies ill in bed upstairs.

And then the child's self-reliant nature asserts

itself. He dares not move his mother, for he knows her weight would overbalance him ; but he snatches up a glass of water and sprinkles some in her face ; and then he runs into the print-shop next door and asks Monsieur Sanson, the pompous printseller, to go quickly for the doctor.

"My mother is very ill, Monsieur Sanson," he says gravely, "and you will do anything for my mother, will you not, neighbour?"

"Yes, yes, my child, I fly—tell your dear mother I am gone."

And Monsieur Sanson, who has an ardent wish to become the stepfather of Eustache, runs off, as fast as his dignity will suffer him, to do the boy's bidding, while Eustache goes back to his mother.

PART II.

MADAME LE CAMAC.

THE cathedral clock has just struck. One—Two—Three —Four, sound loud and deep in the afternoon stillness ; loud and deep enough, one would think, to wake every sleeper in the town—for surely the town itself has gone to sleep in the intensity of this July sunshine.

There is not a sound in the great deserted market-place.   The three inns there show no signs of life, they keep a mysterious stillness behind their green wooden blinds.

There comes presently, at a leisurely pace, across the grass-grown stones of the Place a tall stout priest, his black robes swinging as he walks along.

His face is broad and kindly, red enough just now under the blazing sunshine ; for the big blue umbrella he carries is of too coarse a stuff to afford effectual shelter, the light comes through it and purples his hot cheeks and broad good-tempered nose.

When he reaches the farther side of the great open space he gives a sigh of relief, and turning to the right finds his way up two or three narrow streets to the quiet precincts of the cathedral.

The stately pile is built on the summit of a steep hill, and its spires look down on the valley of the river, and over the monotonous far-stretching plain beyond.

The gray magnificence of architecture and sculptured stone and painted glass is closely girt with houses, so that it is difficult to get far enough away to observe it as a whole.   But Father Cléry is too well acquainted with the beautiful green gray pile to stand considering the relative excellences of the spires, or the

grandeur of the colossal porches, and the perfect carv
ing of some of the eighteen hundred statues which adorn
the building.

He stops before one of the small houses facing the
church, and knocks at the low door.

The door remains closed, but Father Cléry is not
impatient ; the deep cool shadow is delightful, for these
small houses are so close to the cathedral that the sun
never reaches the green paving-stones. It is pleasant to
stand and wipe his hot face with a huge orange pocket-
handkerchief—the only bit of colour besides his own
face and hands in the old gray close.

The door is opening now, and a little slender
woman stands curtseying to Father Cléry. She is very
small and frail-looking, with a delicate pearl-like face,
that tells of faded beauty and of much present sweetness.
Her eyes have been blue—they are pale and clear now
—and the oval face is narrow, and the rounded chin is
much more pointed than it was when we saw her years
ago, but much beauty lingers still in the fine clear skin
and the small expressive mouth, and above all in the
sweet trustful expression that wins hearts at once to
Marie Texier. That expression glows now in the
bright smile with which she greets her visitor.

"Well, my good friend," he says, "and how are

you ? better—ah, that's right ; now having got better, you must keep better—no more fainting-fits—we can't have those, you know ;" he smiles, but Marie looks sorrowful.

" I am very sorry, Father, but I did not know what I did. I was saying my rosary—kneeling in my place—and then on a sudden comes a mist, and then I find myself in the porch, and Madame le Camac throws water in my face "—but a look of shame reddens her face—" pardon me, Father, I keep you standing while I chatter about myself."

The priest smiles.

" It is not often you speak of yourself. I came to-day to bring you news of our boy "—in an instant her eyes have grown dark as the pupils dilate with expectation—" He is settled now," the priest goes on, " he is going to Mont St. Michel in Normandy as soon as there is a vacancy in the community."

The little frail woman grows white in an instant.

" Mont St. Michel, Father. Is it not a prison for rogues and vagabonds, a place cut off from life, far away by the sea ?" her eyes fix wistfully on the priest.

He shrugs his shoulders.

" Of course," he speaks half to himself, " how should you know any better ; a good Catholic like you does not read the newspapers ;" then smiling down into her anxious eyes—" the prison, my daughter, was emptied some years ago ; the prisoners were set free, and the Bishop of Coutances has established a community of priests in the desecrated monastery. I hear that much has already been done to restore and beautify the church. It is a wonderful place," he says reverently, "founded by the holy Archangel himself, as you may read in the sacred legend."

" Yes, Father," but Madame Texier sighs. " Is it more than a hundred kilometres away ?"

" Bah! it is more likely four hundred kilometres away, Marie; but courage, my daughter," for her eyelids droop, and he sees the lashes quiver as if she strove to keep back tears.

" The railway goes as far as Pontorson now, and Pontorson is only a short journey from the Mount—a walk over the sands at low tide. We shall see Eustache here one of these fine days, and he will have stories enough to tell you of the wonders of the Mount. There's no such place in the whole world, Marie ; a rock-convent—rock within and rock without ! why, in the very bowels of the hard stone there is a chapel with a statue of our Lady as black as the blessed Image yonder," he looks over his shoulder at the cathedral.

"Well, well, take care of yourself, and remember, my daughter, that it is an honour to belong to such a wondrous place as Mont St. Michel. Good-day."

He nodded, and then bustled on till he turned out of sight in the direction of the archbishop's palace.

Madame Texier stood looking after him. She had not yet recovered from the shock of his tidings, and she was, for the time, unconscious of time and place; presently she sighed heavily, and went back into her neat room. The pale green panelled walls were very bare; but on one side of the mirror over the fireplace was the photograph of a man of middle age, on the other that of a youth of eighteen, so alike that they might have passed for portraits of the same person—there was in both the same firm mouth, and the same strength and earnestness of expression. The older portrait represented Madame Texier's husband, and the youth was her son, the priest Eustache.

Marie Texier and her husband had loved one another with that true love which death does not end. When her husband died she was still young and pretty, and had a little competence, enough to spare her the need of working for others, and more than one of her fellow-townsmen had urged her to take a second husband. The printseller, Mr. Sanson, had been very importunate ; but they all got the same answer, "Jean Baptiste has gone from our sight—yes—but he is not dead to me ; how could I have two husbands ?"

She was resigned to the loss of this dear friend and companion, but she had never been able to resign herself to one act of her life. She could never tell how she had brought herself to consent that Eustache should enter the priesthood and leave her thus desolate.

" Mother," the boy said, "I will come back one day ; I will say masses in the cathedral ; I shall be close at hand to give you the last offices."   And in the fervour caught from his young devout earnestness Marie had felt capable of any sacrifice ; the parting would not be for long, and then afterwards there would be Eustache always close by—a guide and counsellor as well as a son.   It might be that the reverence and clinging trust she had had for her husband's judgment had transferred themselves to Eustache as he grew each day more and more like his dead father.

And now she sits down in her wooden chair, and thinks how Quixotic and unreal all this seems ; oh, how lonely life is! and how far distant this island convent!   Instinctively she puts her slender hand over her eyes, and finds it wet with tears.

Marie Texier draws her hand away as if a wasp had stung it.

"Holy Virgin, what am I doing? repenting my offering, grudging thee the gift I gave?   No, I do not grudge my boy—my Eustache," and at the name come thronging memories of a rosy baby, of a wee toddler clinging to her skirts, of a bright-eyed acolyte singing with silver treble notes in the choir of the grand old cathedral, last of the pious thoughtful student who, till he went to Bon Secours, used to come over from Paris to spend his holidays with her.   Her heart swells painfully, and tears brim over and fall on the hands that lie clasped in her lap.

She looks up and smiles, "It is not wrong," she says, "so long as I do not murmur.   God permits these tears, or why did He put it in my heart to love my boy so dearly?" and again her tears fall plentifully.

There is a heavy step on the stairs; Madame Texier rises and goes to a tall bureau which faces the front window.   She takes a pocket handkerchief from one of the drawers and wipes her eyes hastily, for the footsteps have reached the lowest stair, and the handle of the door is turning.

There comes in a broad bulky woman garbed in a succession of dark fully plaited woollen skirts, that make her look nearly as broad as she is high. Across a loosely-fitting calico body she wears a brown shawl, its two ends fastened at the back of her waist. Her cap has nothing distinctive about it; it is much like that of Madame Texier, the cap so frequently seen in France on the head of a middle-aged woman of the shopkeeping class—muslin with a close full border round her face, fastened beneath the chin by strings of purple ribbon.   But the face within the cap-border! that indeed is quite another sort of face from Marie Texier's.   Large and square, and coarse and dark; the nose is square - topped and projects, so that it looks like a right angle of flesh set in the midst of this unlovely countenance.   The mouth is enormously wide and lipless, but there are good strong yellow teeth within it.   No vestige of hair shows below the cap, though there is enough on the broad chin to call for a razor; the eyebrows are only faintly indicated, but the eyes though small, are dark and full of kindness.   And yet when Julie le Camac smiles you forget her ugliness, you only say to yourself, " Here is a woman with a heart in her bosom."

She stands an instant in the open doorway, taking in the meaning of Marie Texier's attitude; then she turns her eyes slowly and heavily to the portrait of Jean Baptiste Texier, and shaking her head, her mouth seems to fall open, so listless and inactive is its expression.

" Holy Virgin," she says, " has she then gone back to weeping ?" Julie's shoulders move uneasily. " She who has taught me by her example that I may not weep ; no, it is not that either." Her eyes .nove across to the likeness of Eustache.

Marie Texier has taken her hands from her face, she turns round and tries to smile at her visitor.

Julie shakes her shoulders in a heavy ungainly fashion, more that of an elephant than of a woman.

" If you need your room, Marie, you should speak, I never shrink from hearing a plain truth ;" there is a blundering jocularity in the words, which tells that they do not convey Julie's real meaning.

Madame Texier gazes at her friend with wondering open eyes, she is still too much pre-occupied to look below the surface.

" I need your room ? who says so ?" At this, Julie puts first one short broad-fingered hand to her waist, then the other, and bursts into a loud laugh.

" Ma foi, Marie, you are a daisy still ; you will always be one my poor angel ; well, I won't laugh, because you are not happy ; but if Julie can no longer comfort and help you, then believe me, in all sincerity, it is better for you, my friend, to live with some one who can give you better help, and I have told you often you may well find a score better than such as I am."

There is no hidden meaning in the words. Julie's eyes are full of humble tender love as she looks at her frail little friend.

Madame Texier smiles. "You are very good, neighbour, but you cannot help me to-day. I have heard news that weighs heavily. Eustache is not coming here——he is going farther even than Bon Secours ——he is going to Mont St. Michel; you have heard of the place have you not ?"

Julie stands considering, then a smile breaks slowly over the broad heavy face.

"Yes, I know it ; it is in a picture in the shop of Mr. Sanson next door, but it is only a rock, with a church on the top, and the sea all around. Eustache cannot live there, it is impossible."

"Yes !" and the mother tells Father Cléry's news.

"And he told you all out at once——you who have been ill!" her shoulders touch her ears in scorn, but she refrains from outward blame of the priest.

"Well," she says, when she has listened to the end, "you are not to fret by yourself, Marie Texier ; when you feel tears coming you will come to the stair-foot, and you will say, ' Holà there, Julie, I want to cry ; come down and help me to cry '—why," a look of surprise broadens over her face, " she is laughing at me ; was there ever such a rainbow of a woman ? I wager she will come, if I ask her, and help fresh stuff my mattress ; it is hard to do alone."

Madame Texier smiles, and the two friends go upstairs together.

PART III.

THE PILGRIMAGE.

THERE is a flutter of bustle and excitement over the gray, sleepy, old town, that seems to transform it. The steep streets, winding up and down the side of the hill —so narrow that the quaint gabled top-stories almost touch their opposite neighbours as they overhang the lower part of the ancient stone houses,—are thronged with people all hurrying in one direction, and treading down the grass which shows here and there among the irregular round paving-stones. Follow these hurrying folks and you will come to the pleasant tree-shaded Boulevard on the western side of the town ; the Boulevard which circles the old quarter of the city, and divides it and its picturesque moss-grown irregularities from the modern town, in comparison so clean, so light, and so dull.

Very near the pleasant tree-shaded promenade, so dear to the town dwellers on Sundays and fête-days, is the railway station, and as you get nearer the descent leading to this you notice that many of the hurrying men. women, and children of the throng in which you find yourself carry a bundle or parcel, and in some cases a more ambitious show of luggage in the shape of basket and bag. Some of the old people are clearly not travellers, their hands are empty, except that many of them help their hobbling steps along with a stout stick; the faces of all, whether young or old, are full of a pleasant excitement, and the buzz of tongues increases as the groups cross the Boulevard and go down hill to the railway station.

More than half the number, and these are chiefly women, wear on their shoulders—pinned to the jacket or shawl—a cross of scarlet cloth.

Father Cléry stands at the station gate and welcomes his fellow-travellers as they arrive and pass in one by one. He is to take charge of the Pilgrimage which has been preached for some weeks past at the cathedral and the various churches. His face is full of kindly sympathy with all, and there is a sparkle of eagerness in his eyes, but a glisten comes into them, and his smile is heartier yet, as two women, one small and slender, and one as broad as she is long, come arm and arm down the hill. Madame Texier's delicate face has a rare glow of pleasure on it, and Madame le Camac's dark eyes sparkle, but neither one or other wears the red cross, and the priest smiles when he remarks its absence.

"Good-day," he says heartily, "you are welcome, my daughters. Ah! that is right, Julie, you carry the basket, I see; the strong must help the weak in this work-a-day world; but why have you not put on the badge, my friends? I cannot send in your names as pilgrims without the badge; to all intents and purposes you are pilgrims, and yet you will not reap the benefit our Holy Father offers to those who go on Pilgrimage to the Mount. What say you, Marie? even now it is not too late; Antoine"—he nods his head towards the young deacon who stands near him—"has plenty of crosses in his bag."

Madame Texier curtseys, but she shakes her head.

"I could not feel I was honest," she raises her clear pale eyes to the curé's Face, "for, Father, I had never thought of going to the Mount if my Eustache had stayed at Bon Secours. I am not going on Pilgrimage; I am going to see my boy—once more, only once more, Father, and then I will try to be content."

There was a quiver in her voice that seemed to
Q

trouble Father Cléry, he blew his nose rather noisily before he spoke again.

"Well, and you, Julie," he said, "why should not you wear the cross? you, at any rate, have no son at Mont St. Michel; though, as to that," he turned to Madame Texier, "I say to you as I said before, that chances are against you. The Bishop will be there, all the priests will be in attendance, and, besides, the place will be so thronged with clergy from all parts of France —I may say Europe—that it is more than doubtful whether you find out Eustache in the time we are permitted to remain." He turned sharply to Madame le Camac, whose scanty eyebrows were doing their best to express a frown; "Well, Julie, what is your excuse for not wearing the badge?"

"There is no need for an excuse," one huge shoulder went up awkwardly, and with her free hand she pinched her apron like a shy child. "The good Father knows I cannot leave Marie Texier; if she stays I stay too, if she goes I go, it is simple. I have no son at the Mount the Father says; well, but Marie has one there— it is all the same—ha, ha." She laughed with awkward relief, opening her mouth to such an alarming extent that a stranger, waiting for the same train, drew back aghast that any woman should look so hideous.

Father Cléry smiled.

"Well," he said, "I think you are over scrupulous;" then, as they went on to the waiting-room, he said to the deacon, "I doubt if we have a couple of truer pilgrims among us than those two ; there is no excitement about them, and they will assist at all the offices devoutly. Marie looks better already for the hope of seeing her son."

Meanwhile Madame le Camac was of quite another opinion. She knew how these two years of entire separation had told on the poor little mother, and at first she had tried to dissuade her from the long wearisome journey—for it would be sadly wearisome. Spite of the early hour of starting, the pilgrims would not reach Pontorson till evening—probably too late to go on to the Mount—and it seemed to be uncertain whether they would get lodging for the night even at Pontorson, so many arrivals were expected. But Madame Texier's firm though gentle pleading had prevailed, and Julie had given her consent to the expedition.

"It shall go hard," she said to herself, "if I cannot find a bundle of straw for her to lie on, and I'll undertake to keep her warm."

But the brightness of her friend's eyes and the glow on her cheeks this morning do not deceive Madame le

Camac. She looks wistfully at Marie Texier as they stand wedged in the crowd that more than fills the salle d'attente, and, as the atmosphere grows hot and dense Julie sees her look white and faint.

Just then the door opens, and Father Cléry's tall figure towers behind the little railway official, who pushes in an addition to the closely packed crowd. Julie and her companion are near the door, and Madame le Camac manages to catch the father's eye as he looks smiling over his flock. She points to Madame Texier and opens her huge mouth in dismay. The salle is now so full that it is not easy to open the door widely, but Father Cléry forces a way with his burly shoulders, and the crowd makes a passage for him till he reaches the two women in the corner. "Make way," he says, "bring her into the air," and he leads the way through the buffet to the platform.

Madame Texier draws a deep breath, and then she gives a little frightened glance at Julie, and one full of appeal to the priest.

"I give so much trouble," she says humbly, "and it is quite my own fault—if I roused myself I should not be so silly."

As she speaks a tinge of colour blooms on her cheeks and the priest smiles.

"That is right," he says, "you are getting better. Get her a glass of water, Julie, and keep her walking up and down, and she will soon be herself again."

Madame le Camac is slow-witted, and Father Cléry's quickness is more than she can follow. By the time that she has linked his hopeful words to the faint glow on Marie Texier's face, that glow has faded, and her friend is as white and wan as she was in the hot waiting-room. Madame le Camac's hairless eyebrows draw together thoughtfully, but she cannot find words to say what she wants. At last, very abruptly—so that the words come like stones flung at a window—"Come away, Marie; come, come!"

Madame Texier starts, and looks round in surprise.

"Yes, come away, I have changed my mind ; we will not go to Mont St. Michel."

Such a look of fervour and love comes into the little widow's eyes.

"No, no, Julie, you shall not go—of course you shall not if you do not wish, but I must go, and "—the troubled look on the ugly uncouth face reveals Julie's secret—"my friend, I must go without you ; see then, I hope it is not selfish, but what can I do ? my heart is where my boy is, Julie "—she stops and lays her hand on her bosom—"it draws and draws me to him—

there is more of my life already at the Mount than there is in this poor little body."

She speaks with tender earnestness, for Julie looks sulky; one shoulder is much higher than its fellow, and Madame le Camac fingers the basket in a discontented manner.

" I do not say it is selfish—what do I know; it is perhaps suicide I am helping you to commit, widow Texier."

Julie will not look at her friend ; her eyes are fixed on a line of baggage trucks opposite.

Madame Texier smiles sadly. She knows that Julie only calls her widow Texier when she is really displeased. She puts her hand timidly on the big square shoulder.

" Listen, kind friend.   It is not only for myself—it is more," she looks round to see that no one is near, " far more for my Eustache—he does not say he pines for me,—my boy is too good to ask the slightest fatigue or expense from his mother,—but there is a longing one can feel through words, a sadness that speaks without complaint. Mon Dieu! I hope it is not all for myself; but indeed, my good Julie, I think the sight of me will put a great joy into the heart of my Eustache."

Her voice trembles, and Julie rubs her eyes roughly with her hand.

"Well," she says harshly, "and when your visit is paid, what then? will it not be worse for you both to part again?"

Marie Texier smiles.

"Who knows," she says brightly, "I may find a lodging at the Mount," then, touched by the dismay shown by the gaping mouth and widely-opened eyes, "but why look on so far; the day is enough to live through, and we shall not reach Mont St. Michel to-day, my good Julie."

PART IV.

OVER THE SANDS.

THE rain has fallen in torrents through the night; it has soaked through many of the half-roofed sheds in which the tired pilgrims had been glad to lie down and sleep when they reached Pontorson, so that they rise up with wet garments.

Madame le Camac stands at the door of the café where, thanks to Father Cléry, she and Marie Texier have found a lodging, and Julie congratulates herself that her friend has been thus sheltered.

The wind, too, has risen during the night, and it howls dismally as it rushes through the old grey town to the waste of far stretching sand, for it is neap-tide at the Mount, and there is no fear of shifting sands to-day. Still, Father Cléry has arranged that the pilgrims shall start early, so that they may be in time for High Mass, and may be able to return to Pontorson before dark. The journey has already cost a large sum, and they must go on foot to the Mount itself, walking in Pilgrimage across the far-stretching waste of sand.

As the distance is six miles or so, a rough cart has been secured for the weaker members of the flock, and in this jolting springless vehicle Father Cléry has found a place for Marie Texier.

Madame le Camac cannot stay to help her friend in, for the walking procession is to start first, and the priest and his colleagues find it hard work to place their pilgrims in suitable order before they begin their journey to the Mount. It is a dismal expedition ; the procession leaves the old town and moves slowly on by the uneven road towards the river till it reaches the borders of the Gréve. The dreary waste of sand stretches itself out in weird vastness, and far away, mingled with the driving mass of gray cloud, is the shadowy Mont St. Michel, its outline blurred by the torrent of rain that still falls.

The cart in which Marie Texier rides has got alongside of the other pilgrims, and Marie puts her hand over her eyes so as to get a clearer view of the church planted high among the clouds.

"My Eustache," she murmurs softly, "my dear boy, thank God I shall see him at last."

How far off the Mount looks, and how impossible it seems that there can be any dwellers on that shadowy rock that looms out from the desolate waste of tawny sand, and seems to mingle with the storm-clouds. On the right, far away, crouching on the dull drab-coloured sand, the huge dark rock Tombelaine looks like a lion about to spring ; one might fancy him the storm-fiend keeping watch over the howling wind and rising waves. In the distance far behind is the Mount, right and left of it the gray sea stretches far and wide. One of her fellow-pilgrims watches the wonder in Marie's gazing eyes.

"At the great tides," he says, "the waves roll up to the very foot of the wall that surrounds Mont St. Michel. and it is cut off completely from land."

Their fellow-pilgrim is an old man with flowing white hair ; he has already visited the Mount, and he shakes his head sadly, and points out to Marie a spot made dangerous by the quicksands. A cross stands near it telling of past woe. "But, indeed," the white-haired pilgrim says, "except at neap-tide, such as we have now, when there is no fear of the return of the water, it is very dangerous to cross the sands without a guide."

All at once the rain ceases, and suddenly, distinct before them, as though a veil had suddenly lifted, is the bourne of the Pilgrimage, the Mont St. Michel. A glad cry passes along the band, and led by Father Cléry they chant a hymn in honour of the Holy Archangel.

"Ah!" says the fellow-traveller, "once on a time there was a golden statue of the saint on the summit of the church ; now there is a weathercock."

"Are people often lost on the sands?"

Marie shivers and draws her shawl closely round her as she asks.

"*Dame*, no. There are seldom new-comers dwelling at the Mount, and those who go from the continent do not venture unwarily on the sands. One was lost not long ago, however ; he was a priest."

Marie's hands tremble till her shawl almost slips from them. "Was he young, monsieur?" she says. "Did you hear where he came from?"

"Not I."

Marie's lip quivers ; she says a prayer to herself. If it should be so ! Eustache has not written to her for many weeks, not even in answer to the letter in which she announced her coming. But, no: she will not listen to a vague fear. She will trust and hope, and as the Mount comes nearer and more and more distinct, hope and trust become easier.

The wind has been rising higher and higher, and suddenly it swoops down in a whirling gust on the tired band of travellers. The fellow-traveller cries out and clutches at his hat; he is too late, it has taken flight and is sailing on the furious blast. The pilgrims scatter over the sands, and struggle wildly against the gale, while their hats fly like black ants into gray distance, farther and farther away.

"Stop there; halt, come back! I command you." Father Cléry's hat has flown with the rest, and he runs after it too, but soon he stops, very red and panting.

"It is useless, my friends," he cries; "come back. In our eagerness we shall lose the track, and plunge, for aught I know, into some unsafe ground." Then he adds with a laugh, "We may hope for an extra blessing on bare-headed pilgrims."

And after some delay the Father gets his scattered flock together again.

PART IV.

AT THE MOUNT.

THERE are five hundred pilgrims in Mont St. Michel
to-day, without counting many visitors and tourists who
do not wear the red cross.   The inns are full and over-
flowing, and up in the fortress abbey there are large
fires blazing on the enormous stone hearths of the
refectory, and cooking is going on as if the old monastic
hospitality were once more revived.   Covers are laid on
the long wooden tables, and the tariff of prices is
moderate : but the viands do not look as tempting as
they do down at the Lion d'Or, near the entrance gate
of the rocky town.

There is a rare bustle at the Lion d'Or to-day.   Its
low-roofed kitchen, into which you step down from the
street, has few windows, and as the entrance door is
small the kitchen is dark within.   A young priest stands
at the door asking questions, and as he looks inside the
scene seems too picturesque for reality.   Little by little
his eyes grow accustomed to the darkness, and he sees
more than one long table filled with pilgrims, eating,
drinking, laughing, joking, growing every moment noisier
and merrier, each wearing the scarlet cross.

LA MERVEILLE, MONT ST.-MICHEL.

The young priest steps down into the rambling black-beamed place, and scans curiously the faces of its inmates, but a push on his arm disturbs his scrutiny.

He stands with his back to a large wood fire on the open hearth, and as he looks round, a stout comely woman pushes her way up to the burning logs. She is clad in blue woollen, and her bare, plump, outstretched arms carry a huge frying-pan full of broken eggs.

" By your leave, my reverend," she says. " This is the omelette for the company upstairs, and they must not be kept waiting for it."

The young priest looks at the golden mass. There must be, in the frying-pan, at least thirty eggs, he thinks. There are, then, other pilgrims upstairs. And he climbs the creaking steps which rise from the kitchen itself.

In the room upstairs are three tables full of guests, but not one face that he seeks, and the priest comes sadly downstairs again, just as the smoking golden omelette is being carried up. The mistress gives it to her deft waitress, and then she smiles at the priest.

" Well, monsieur," she says, " it is not well of the fathers at the convent to be cheating us of our dues ; you cannot cook—you had better tend the sick. I hear there was a poor woman taken ill this morning, and no doctor could be got for her."

" A sick woman," he says eagerly. " I wish I had

known.   No, the doctor is absent ; he went to Avranches this morning.   Where is this sick woman ?"

" *Ma foi !* how can I know ?"—she puts both hands to her head—"I remember nothing to-day but my orders."   She adds, laughing, " My husband there will tell you ; he has nothing to do but to talk," she smiles with a touch of sarcasm on her comely face, " nothing but to sit there talking," she points to a table at the back of the great rambling kitchen.   Mine host, in a brown holland blouse, sits here smoking a prodigious pipe. with about six red-faced companions, also in blouses. There is a great cider pitcher on the table, and, judging by the faces of the host and his companions, it has been emptied and refilled more than once.

As the priest approaches, the host looks up with a sort of careless indifferenee.

" Can you tell me "—the young man is disgusted at what seems to him at such a time profane excess— " you, monsieur, I mean," this is said more sharply, for the innkeeper has not even removed his pipe, " where the sick pilgrim I hear of has been removed to ?"

The innkeeper lays down his long pipe and smiles.

" *Dame !*" he shrugs his shoulders ; " there is not much amiss, she will do well enough.   I was by when she fainted at the gate here this forenoon, but just now

André said he saw her in the procession with the rest of the Chartres pilgrims waiting for the Bishop."

" Chartres pilgrims, did you say ?" The young priest starts, and then flushes ; his voice is very eager. " Are you not mistaken. The pilgrims to-day are surely from Versailles and Tours."

" From Versailles, yes, reverend father, but not from Tours. Father Gaspard told me this morning that the Tours pilgrims have not yet reached Pontorson, and these from Chartres have come to-day in place of them."

. But before the last words are spoken the priest has turned to go away. He hurries out of the inn, passes through the dark archway of the inner battlement, and then, turning aside from the crooked street of ancient stone houses, goes up the steep ascent to the fortress abbey. The rain has ceased, but the wind howls yet more wildly over the waste ; a waste even more dismal here, for it seems boundless, except where a faint blue line marks the Breton coast, and on the right a stronger, nearer line of margin traces out Avranches and the Norman sea-board.

Farther north, islands make uncertain specks in the wide expanse of gray sea and monotonous gréve, for at this height the variation of tint is indiscernible, and the infinite sameness gives a weird melancholy to the prospect —a melancholy that fills the heart with unaccustomed throbbings and fragments of thought, fragments which might—who can say?—grow into poetry in a longer contemplation.   The young priest had felt these throbbings on his first arrival at the Mount, but to-day, though the atmosphere was charged with weird pathos, he hurried on, alike unmindful of the desolate waste or of the superb "marvel" of masonry before him, till he stopped at last before the frowning doorway and entered the monastery.

In the guard-room two priests were busy at one end of the large vaulted hall, selling crosses and rosaries to pilgrims, while at the other end some peasant-women had set up a shop for photographs.

"You must hasten," one of these said to her customer, "or you will miss the benediction in the Crypte des Gros Piliers.   The Bishop is on his way there now."

"Do you hear, Adèle," the woman who was buying said to her companion ; "hasten, or we shall miss another sight."   They paid hastily for their purchases, and scrambled up the steps which led into the interior of the building.

Here all was scramble and confusion ; the ordinary guides were making holiday, and people roamed aimlessly up and down the long passages and dark irregular flights of stone steps, trying to find their way to the crypt, and fearing to lose themselves and to get buried out of hearing in some of the far-off world-famous dungeons of the fortress abbey. A few dim oil-lamps here and there only shed a faint glimmer in the utter darkness of the place round the spot on which they hung—stone walls and roof alike black with age.

But the priest knew his road, and he hurried on through the noisy groups of pilgrims till he reached the chapel of Notre Dame-sous-Terre.

He had purposely avoided the main entrance to the crypt, and had gone in at the side, and now he stood wedged in by the crowd against one of the groups of huge pillars which give its name to this wonderful chapel, or series of five chapels, beneath the church itself.

Even his eager search for the Chartres pilgrims was checked for an instant by the scene. A little way from him was the famous image, a black Madonna, richly dressed and surrounded by a wreath of flowers ; over her head hung a lamp, shining out like a star against the dark pillar and black vaulted roof, while from the roof itself hung an iron chandelier filled with blazing candles. The spaces between the two circles of pillars were inky in their depth of darkness.

Just under the chandelier, so that the light concentrated itself on his gold jewelled mitre and splendid vestments, stood the tall Bishop of Coutances, his jewelled crosier borne beside him ; behind and around, stretching away into the dark aisles, was a crowd of white-robed priests and acolytes, and beyond these again, surging round the crypt till every inch of it was filled, so closely packed that it seemed as if you might walk on their bowed heads or upturned faces, were the pilgrims ; each of them was marked with the red cross, and many of them carried a lighted candle.

And now the Bishop began the hymn, and as the pilgrims poured out their voices till the sound rang from arch to arch, and, swelling out through the dark arches, was echoed back from far-distant seldom-trodden galleries, tears rolled down many of the withered cheeks, and fell on many starched cap-strings and many a ragged gray beard.

The hymn swelled louder and louder, and then, as it ended abruptly, the procession formed itself and began slowly to leave the underground chapel. Just as the Bishop turned to follow the long string of priests, there was a swaying movement in the crowd, and a woman's voice cried :

"Make way—make way, I tell you. You will trample on her ; see, she is falling !"

"Mon Dieu !" an old gray-bearded man wheezes out. " She should not be in such a crowd ; folks come here to worship, not to faint."

The priest has pushed his way through the swaying, moving mass, and now he stands beside the woman who cried out just now. Well enough he knows that hugely-opened mouth and that triangular nose, but he has no time to recognise Madame le Camac. His eyes go on to the burden she struggles to keep from falling, for her arm is clasped closely round her small slender companion. The priest does not stop to gaze at that gray death-like face, nor does he ask a question.

"Leave her—make way," he says, as he bends over Marie Texier, and raises her in his strong young arms. He bears her out of the dark chapel, along a passage to a staircase, and Julie scrambles after him quickly, and finds herself presently in a square cloister, three hundred feet high in air, surrounded on all its sides with exquisite lancet arches, supported on slender sculptured columns.

The priest has lain his burden down just within these arches, he kneels beside Marie and unties her cap-strings.

Madame le Camac is bustling forward, but at the agony in the priest's face she stops short, for she recognises Eustache. The little mother and her boy are together at last. The mother's eyes are open now; she too sees her boy, and a bright smile shines out of the wan gray face. Julie shrinks back and cowers behind the arches. Too well she knows the joy that fills that tender long-suffering heart ; how could she rob it of one minute of its longed-for happiness ? She must yield up her part in Marie now. So she shrinks out of sight.

"Mother, mother," Eustache says, "how long has this been ? Oh, why did I not know ?" for too surely it seems to him that death hovers on that ashy face and on those purple lips.

His mother gazes fondly at him, and tries to put up her hand and stroke his face.

"My Eustache," so softly said that he has to lean down to hear, "it is I who should kneel to him for blessing." Her eyes close. "Thank God," she whispers as he stoops to kiss her forehead.

"Mother, you will recover." He looks round for help, and he sees the figure crouching behind the slender columns.

"Some water from the sacristy !" He points to a large doorway up some steps. "Send one of the convent fathers," he says, hurriedly.

Poor Julie ! She gives one sad hungering look to the spot where Marie lies. It is too hard. She, whose whole life's happiness lies there fading quickly away, she must leave her, and give up the hope of a last farewell, while Eustache—— "Oh, it is hard ; it is hard. He left her of his own free will," she says, hurrying along ; " he has been happy enough without her all this while—but, Holy Virgin, I am wicked !" And she goes on still more quickly.

And while she hurries on, Eustache says all this to himself. " I have been happy without her—yes," he says ; " but, oh, mother, I have sorely longed for thee ! Mother—little mother, speak to me—one word !" He forgets all. He is no longer the calm, self-sustained priest Eustache ; his hot tears are falling on the pale face.

" Has it been worth while ?" he murmurs ; and then, after a long, silent pause, with bowed head, he sobs, " Oh, mother, how thy loving heart has ached for me !"

Heavy steps come along the cloister. He starts, looks up, and here are Father Cléry and Julie side by side.

The young priest clasps his mother in his arms, as if he fears she will be taken from him ; but Father Cléry bends down and looks in her face for an instant ; then he draws back, and gently draws back the eager Julie. " Hush !" he says, reverently, "we are too late. All that is left us now is to say the office for the faithful departed."

CHAPTER XI.

THE CASTLE OF FALAISE—ARLETTE—HONFLEUR—PONT-AUDEMER
—THE FOUROLLE—BESIDE THE RILLE.

FROM Avranches we went on to Vire, and thence the diligence drive to Caen is one of the most charming incidents of Norman travel. We had stayed in Caen before, and so we did not linger in the old city, so rich in churches, and in associations specially interesting to English men and women. We were anxious to visit the castle and town of Falaise—the birthplace of William the Bastard.

The town of Falaise is built on the top of a lofty platform, the extremity of which is a precipice (whence the name Falaise). From this rocky termination of the platform rise, sheer and frowning, the imposing ruins of the castle, consisting of the Norman donjon-keep and Talbot's tower, the last a noble piece of masonry, built by the famous Englishman Talbot, warden of the Norman marches.

Henry V. of England besieged this castle in 1418.

BIRTHPLACE OF WILLIAM THE CONQUEROR.

It withstood him for four months.   Between 1418 and 1450 Talbot built the tower which bears his name ; it is more than a hundred feet high, and the walls are fifteen feet in thickness; there are four stories in it, of which the floors remain ; a winding stair leads to the roof, from whence is a magnificent view.   The Castle of Falaise was besieged by Henri Quatre in 1559.   It held out against his cannon for only seven days, and the breach in the wall by which he took the castle by assault still remains.   Altogether, this fortress has sustained nine sieges, one from William the Conqueror himself when quite a lad.

At the foot of the rocky height from which the castle rises winds the river Ante, pleasantly shaded by trees.   Beside the stream are the washing-places of the townswomen, as they also were in the far-off days of the Norman Duke.

The legend relates that one day, looking out of a window of the lofty castle keep, Robert Count of Hiesmes, afterwards Duke Robert the Magnificent, saw Arlette washing clothes in the river Ante.   She was very beautiful, and the youth at once fell in love with her. Arlette was the daughter of a tanner of the town, and neither daughter nor father seems to have held out long against the young Count's love and importunity.

The son born to Robert and Arlette was the future conqueror of England, born in the castle,—so says tradition,—and a little room is still shown as "Arlette's Bower."

The Count of Hiesmes is said to have always treated his lowly love with the greatest tenderness and consideration. After his death Arlette married Herlwin of Conteville. Two sons were the fruits of this marriage —both destined to be celebrated, though in a less degree than their half-brother William—Odo, Archbishop of Bayeux, and Robert, Earl of Cornwall.

From Falaise to Mezidon, and thence to Honfleur, is an easy journey, and there is something in Honfleur which made us go back there willingly, although we had already passed through it after leaving Etretat. Poor Honfleur was once queen of the Seine, and its famous port held complete command across the mouth of the fair river. In those days it boasted 17,000 inhabitants, and now perhaps it does not possess 1000, for the far more modern city of Havre has taken all the wind out of its sails, and mud has choked its harbour. It still sends quantities of fruit, butter, and eggs to England, and the apricots of Honfleur are renowned.

Many of the old wooden houses are picturesque, and the market-place is very quaint, as the illustration

shows. But the great attraction is the charming walk
up the shady side of a hill looking over the Seine to

MARKET-PLACE, HONFLEUR.

the pilgrimage chapel of Notre-Dame de Grace, and
the view from the Calvary here is most striking.

The chapel is very interesting, full of votive offerings of sailors who have escaped shipwreck, and of others about to embark on a long voyage.

Around Honfleur, and more especially between Havre and Caudebec, a pleasant feature of the country is the Norman farm-house, embosomed in orchards with thatched roof and neatly-kept barns, in great contrast to its Breton neighbours, where pigs roam freely where they please, and where the corn is threshed by hand in the farm-yard, or outside the house-door ; but spite of these evidences of civilisation, superstitions are as rife in Normandy as they are in Brittany, especially in the neighbourhood of Pont-Audemer, where the belief in fourolles is firmly established.   The fourolle is a woman who has committed sacrilege, and for this sin is doomed for seven years to wander at night as a will o' th' wisp. She does not seem to have the power of working as much mischief as the feu-follet, who is supposed to be a sinful priest, but she is doomed to wander, terrifying and terrified by travellers.   If any one addresses the fourolle by her real name, while she is dreeing her penance, her term of seven years begins once again.

The drive between Honfleur and Pont-Audemer is charming, full of beauty and special points of interest, and it was while taking this drive that we learned the tradition of the fourolle.

A NORMAN FARM-HOUSE.

Beside the Rille.

A LEGEND OF PONT-AUDEMER.

CHAPTER I.

A FENCING MATCH.

MADEMOISELLE LOUIS COURBON has a very thoughtful look on her fair freckled face, and her round green eyes have a sadness in them that is quite unusual; for Mademoiselle, although no longer young, is as merry as ever she was, and her plump, round, little well-dressed figure and smiling face are always to be found when amusement is going on in Pont-Audemer. Her round very green eyes are puzzlers : sometimes they are full of innocent open wonder, and then they give through the half-shut yellow eye-lashes long glances, which can only be called furtive. She is an orphan, but her parents left her that little half-timbered tumbledown house beside the Rille, with its gable atop and washing-place below. This last is a source of revenue, for the river washes the basements of the multiform picturesque dwellings beside it, and Louise lets out the washing-shed to about twenty-laundresses, a set of merry hard-working souls, as diligent at blackening their neighbours' characters as they are at soaping their linen.

Louise ekes out her slender income by dressmaking ; that is to say, she will make dresses, and bonnets and caps also, for a chosen few. She works for Madame C., the wife of that citizen who celebrated his retirement from the office of mayor by building, on the top of the steep green hill which closes in one end of the town, the staring white house which "swears" — as the natives say — with everything else in Pont-Audemer ; she has also worked for Madame Trajon, the wife of the lawyer and town-clerk ; and for old friendship's sake she now and then makes a gown for the handsomest girl in Pont-Audemer, Françoise Gérard. But this is a condescension ; the dressmaker considers Françoise her equal; and it is not for the girl's sake that she makes the gowns, but for that of Louis Perreyve, a young soldier, far away now, whom Louise loves as though he were her young brother.

Louise Courbon is in a hurry to-day, and so, instead of lingering beside the lovely Rille—merry with its shedfuls of chattering, laughing washerwomen, noisy with the whirr of the bark-mills which show beside the stream, among the quaint half-timbered and red-brick houses backed by lofty poplar-trees, the green hill rising above them all—we must go on with her along the quay

—for Louise has crossed the bridge, and there is a stone-bordered quay on this side the water, with little flights of steps, up which girls come slowly, so as not to upset the tall well-shaped brown pitchers poised on their heads.

Half-way along the quay Louise turns on the right into a small narrow street, and crosses the bridge in the middle of it. On each side of the canal—for here is one of the many branches of the poor hard-worked river Rille—old tumbledown wooden houses go down to the water's edge, reflecting their grim and scarred old faces in the stream, with here and there bright flowered nasturtium wreaths clinging to the old gray boards or moss-grown tiles.

The water is low to-day, for a dark line and a growth of tiny creeping plants on the foundations of the old houses show that it is sometimes a foot or so higher, and at such high tides the white-capped woman who is now kneeling on a flat stone, and beating the red shirt under her hands so vehemently with her wooden bat, would surely be under water if she tried to wash in the river as it flows by her house. At the back window of one of the houses on the left Louise sees a face she knows, and begins to nod. Then, instead of following the street to its end on the market-place, she takes a narrow turning on the left, parallel with the quay and also with the Grande Place below.

She looks yet more serious as she stops at a door, and then, after knocking, enters.

"Go into the front parlour, Mademoiselle," a welcoming voice says from a room at the back ; "be kind enough to wait, and I am with you directly."

The welcoming voice has a fat wheezy sound, and Mademoiselle Louise's face is yet graver.

"Wicked old hypocrite !" she says, her freckled face growing white with anger—a greenish white, which does not beautify Mademoiselle—"giving herself such airs, too !" and then she looks round the room with a sigh of envy, for small as it is there is no room like it in Pont-Audemer.

The floor is very dark and highly polished, so that even well-practised Mademoiselle Louise walks thereon with caution. The panelled walls, painted a bluish white, and the white lace curtains, are like the walls and curtains of many another house in Pont-Audemer ; but where else will you see such a richly carved oak-beam across the ceiling, or such a fine sculptured mantelshelf, or find such carved oak chests and cabinets of different shape and size, but all manifestly genuine antiques and in good preservation ? Truth to tell, their owner is a dealer in such works. There is a chest of Louis Treize period, with a " Last Supper " carved thereon, that any connoisseur must long to possess, and on one of the others, a tall narrow bit of rich carving shaped like a what-not, are three tall Venice glasses with flower-shaped bells and slender-twisted stems. There is a wealth of colour in these old glasses, gold and blue, green and opal, full of all hues, and softening all. A Persian rug in front of the fireplace, glowing with rich colour, makes the faded blue curtains which screen the hearth yet more faint in hue, for though it is autumn the weather is still warm at Pont-Audemer.

On a small oak table in the middle of the room are some admirable photographs in standing frames, and in the centre of these is a glassful of exquisite flowers—myrtle and jessamine.

" It must be the miller who gives these flowers," says Louise, with a very sour look on her usually good-natured mouth. " He has come to gifts, then, already, has he ? I am not one day too soon if I want to help Françoise. I'll see if I cannot be one too many for Mother Thérèse."

There is a gasping noise in the passage, but no sound of footsteps.

" She creeps about like a mouse, sly old toad," says

the irate dressmaker; "I know her ways; she shall not catch me tripping."

And she plants herself at the door, her eyes round with innocent wonder.

"Be welcome then, my good friend," the wheezy waddling dame says, as she appears, and her florid brick-dust coloured face is creased with a smile, which somehow always has the effect of a grin in the small black twinkling eyes of Madame Gérard. She is fat and round and smiling, but she is not genial-looking, her small keen eyes are set too near, and look across one another, her lips are thin and colourless, and as she has lost her front teeth, her tongue shows in a disfiguring manner when she laughs. She wears a black silk dress, and a cap trimmed with lace and purple ribbon, and her hands are small and soft, in spite of their wrinkles. "You are just the person I need. I have a nice dress, Mademoiselle, and it will be charming if you will only consent to make it up for me."

Louise's round eyes change in an instant to green slits, but she forces a smile to her lips.

"Oh, but you ask me an impossibility, Madame Gérard. What can I do? I refuse the wife of Simon the butcher. I refuse Madame Fouquier of the Grande

Rue. I have indeed refused Madame Mousseline herself at the Pot-d'Acier. What can I do? I offend all the rest of my neighbours if I work for one and refuse the others."

While her visitor speaks, Madame Gérard has waddled to the old yellow sofa, and she pats the wide seat with her little brown hand as an invitation to Mademoiselle Louise.

"Bah,"—for the dressmaker has stopped for breath —"who are all these people? You will not surely confound me—the widow of a distinguished artist— with the wives of the butcher and grocer, or with Madame Mousseline of the Pot-d'Acier. I should think not, indeed!" She rubs her hands together, and there is malice in her little black eyes.

Up go Louise's shoulders in a shrug that brings them near her ears. She feels spiteful, and a red spot glows in each cheek. "An artist!" she says to herself; "that is not much. But Gérard was not even an artist; he made photographs, and bought old furniture." Then, to Madame Gérard: "It is all the same, Madame, these ladies consider you their equal. You see we do not always estimate ourselves rightly. However, at present I am busier than I care to be," she adds with dignity.   Then, in a tone of forced care-lessness, " Is Françoise at home ?"

Madame Gérard's face does not change, but her small eyes are full of war.

" Yes, yes ! the dear child is at home, but she is busy.   I will give her any message, Mademoiselle Louise."

Instead of answering, Mademoiselle Courbon, who has remained standing, runs out of the room to the foot of the stairs, crying, " Françoise, Françoise, where are you ?"

Madame Gérard waddles along the passage as fast as she can go, but Louise is already half-way up the old-fashioned staircase.

On the landing she pauses, half-strangled, for a young girl has sprung down the upper flight and flung both arms round her friend's neck.

" Come down," she says, " why should you have the trouble of climbing, Louise ?"

" Yes, yes, come down ! " in a gasping shriek from below, for Madame Gérard has reached the foot of the stairs.

" Françoise,"—Louise looks up at her tall elegant friend with angry eyes—" I want to talk to you alone, let us go up."

But tall strong Françoise has put both hands on her little friend's shoulders, and she pushes her towards the lower flight.

"No, not to-day," she smiles; "how can I disobey my mother, Louise?"

At this Louise's eyes contract, and she gives a green gleam at the handsome wilful creature who has so suddenly remembered her obedience. She keeps silence, however, till they are all three in the parlour again.

"Is it true, Françoise, this that I hear," impetuously, "that you are letting yourself be courted by Emile Constant?"

The dark-eyed, dark-browed girl bends her head and twists her long fingers together. Her mother's eyes twinkle keenly.

"Good Louise, you doubt no one, you believe all you hear. What sweet innocence at your age!"

Louise turns her back on Madame Gérard's smiles. "I wait an answer from you, Françoise," she says.

Françoise has handsome features, brilliant eyes, and good dark hair; but she has a pale sallow skin, and now this is becoming suffused with red, and she looks abject and ready to cry.

"Monsieur Constant," she says fretfully, "yes, he

comes to see us.   Mother, you said there was no harm in his visits ; why don't you tell Louise so ?"

The little dressmaker takes firm hold of the twining fingers, and fixes her eyes on the confused face.   She sees a struggle in it, but she cannot be sure what this means; she fears by a word even to injure the cause she has come to plead, and yet she must speak.

"Would Louis Perreyve like to hear of Monsieur Constant's visits ?" she says in a low voice.

It is unfortunate that Louise is so short, for Françoise sees over her the shakes of the head and the expressive frowns of that wonderfully placid-faced mother ; it is very curious that out of such a flat shapeless lump of flesh such rapid flashes can emanate. Those little restless eyes do it all, though perhaps the lipless wide mouth gives force and a kind of cruelty to the sharp glances.

Françoise tosses her head.

"Louis is not a tyrant, and he would say I was impertinent if I objected to my mother's visitors."

Louise squeezes the girl's fingers till she hurts them.   Madame Gérard tries to put in her word, but the little woman will not be stopped.

"Listen ;" as the girl pulls her hands away, Louise turns suddenly and stands sideways between mother and daughter. " I'll do nothing underhand ; but remember, Madame Gérard, you let your girl promise herself to Louis Perreyve in my presence, and but for old Eustache you would have let her marry him too. Well then, because Eustache Perreyve has lost his money and Louis will be a poor man, is he to be cast off for a rich new comer like Emile Constant ?. Shame on you, Thérèse Gérard."

Madame Gérard snaps her fingers in Louise's face.

" Shame on you, you meddler. What call have you to be keeping guard over a fine girl like Françoise, with a mother to protect her ? But single women are all alike : they think every chance a girl gets is so much taken from themselves. I suppose you have an eye to Monsieur Constant."

Louise keeps her eyes fixed on Françoise's face. She smiles scornfully at the last words.

" Well, Madame, I have done my part ; but when Monsieur Constant comes to Pont-Audemer again I shall tell him all I know. He is not one to be content with another man's leavings."

CHAPTER II.

A FOUROLLE.

PONT-AUDEMER is a small town.   It has a large, grand
old church, and a large market-place ; besides this
there is one long street, the Grande Rue, with the country
rising up in a green hill at each end, and the street in
which Louise lives, on each side of the Rille, which
runs through it ; besides these there are little narrow
turnings which connect the two wide streets and traverse
the canals which work the tan-mills.   On this account,
as every one sees every one else at church or in the
market, news spreads quickly in Pont-Audemer.

Louise Courbon knows this well, and she says to
herself as she walks home :—

"If Emile Constant did not live all by himself at
Montfort, he would have known long ago that Françoise
is promised to Louis Perreyve."

But to-morrow is market morning, and it is quite
possible for Louise to walk beside the river on the way
to Montfort, and meet Monsieur Constant as he goes to
market.

"I will tell him Françoise is promised, and I will
tell him something else—something you do not quite
count on, Mother Thérèse."

OLD HOUSES, PONT-AUDEMER.

Next morning is full of drizzling rain, the river looks a dull gray as she walks beside it, and the leaves of the poplar-trees hang down heavily—they are so wet that they scarcely tremble on their slender stems.

Almost as she leaves her house, some one comes limping along and takes off his cap to Louise—a tall stiff-looking man in a blouse and canvas trousers. He does not wear a beard, but his long gray moustaches give him a military aspect, and he is truly an old soldier of the First Napoleon ; but his lameness disqualified him early, and he earns a peaceful living as a gardener at Pont-Audemer.

"Good-morning, Monsieur Perreyve," Louise nods and smiles ; "is there any news of Louis ?"

"Good-day, Louise ; there is no news of my boy, and I hear he is going to the frontier, so there is no hope of seeing him perhaps for months ; but where are you off to so early, my beauty ?"

He shuts one eye and laughs slily ; he has no idea of making fun of Louise—to him she is always the young fresh girl of seventeen who grew old and staid all in one night when the news came that Gaspard Perreyve, Louis' eldest brother, had fallen in Algeria, fighting bravely. The news killed Madame Perreyve, and Louise set aside her own grief to comfort the widower and his son Louis, then a boy of ten years old.

Louise looks round sharply, and a tinge of colour spreads over her freckled face.

"You should take care, Monsieur Perreyve ; it is better to pay a compliment in-doors."

"Ah, mon Dieu, is she not original !"—he bursts into a peal of laughter, and at last he pulls off his cap and takes out of it a yellow and blue handkerchief, with which he wipes his eyes. "A compliment !" he murmurs amid his laughter. "Ma foi, but she is original."

Louise has something more to say, and she gets impatient as he breaks into fresh laughter, and puts her hand rather firmly on his arm.

"But, my friend, do listen : I say it is a pity Louis does not come home to look after Françoise."

"Mille tonnerres !"—he leaves off laughing and looks as blustering as if he still wore a uniform ; Louise knows him too well to trust him further—he has no discretion, this simple old gardener, and he would be capable of walking up to Emile Constant on the Grande Place and boxing his ears, if he were told that the miller had dared to visit his son's betrothed.

"Good-day," she nods and smiles, and hurries on at a pace which she knows poor limping Eustache cannot attempt.

The river takes a bend, and she is soon out of sight of the houses. It is a lovely walk, spite of the drizzling rain, but Louise is absorbed in looking out for the rich miller of Montfort.

Here he comes at last on a tall gray horse, which he sits so as to resemble one of his own corn sacks.

Louise has never spoken to him, but that does not stand in her way. She knows him well enough by sight—has she not lately watched him come out four times from the house of Mother Thérèse? Louise drops a curtsey as he comes up to her.

On nearer inspection, Monsieur Constant looks rather like a pudding with a dumpling atop—or perhaps like a home-baked loaf; his face is pale and round, he wears a large round straw hat and a brown holland blouse; he has staring dull blue eyes and a small round mouth, and these features open widely when Mademoiselle Courbon curtseys. He takes off his hat, but his curiosity will not suffer him to pass on.

"Your servant, Mademoiselle. You are doubtless an inhabitant of Pont-Audemer, whose acquaintance I have yet the pleasure to make."

"The pleasure is not certain, Monsieur"—Louise speaks carelessly; as a short woman, she has a natural contempt for this stout pigmy on the tall gray horse; "but I have to make you, Monsieur, acquainted with

some matters, and as they are private, it seems to me
you had better get down and hear them."

Where the miller's eyebrows should be, thick red
semicircles rise towards the roots of his scanty hair,
his eyes glance mournfully towards his little gaitered
legs, and the corners of his mouth droop as much as is
possible.

" Mademoiselle." he says, puffing out each word as
if blowing soap bubbles, " I am enchanted to receive
your confidences, but—but it is difficult for me to
descend without assistance—and—I might injure my
legs."

Louise sneers till her nose turns up more than
ever.

" Don't be afraid," she says ; " I'll hold your horse,
and you can lean on my shoulder."

"Ah—you—are very kind—Mademoiselle," he puffs
more than ever, but he sits still in his saddle.

" Mademoiselle"—he looks slowly round and then
settles himself comfortably—" I see no one but the
ducks in the river ; if you will have the complaisance
to stand close beside me I will bend down as much as
possible"—he propels out each word—"and I will thus
receive your information.   Ahem."

" Little fool," Louise thinks ; but she is too anxious

to lose more time, and seeing that Constant has grown purple in the effort to bend down towards her, she goes close up to the horse.

"Monsieur," she says gravely, "are you not courting Mademoiselle Françoise Gérard?"

Monsieur sits suddenly upright.

"I—I—I—by what right, Mademoiselle, do you ask me such a question?"

"Right?"—Louise is puzzled for a moment. "Well, Monsieur, if I saw a man robbing you of your handkerchief I should cry out, and you would thank me instead of asking for my right; but I forget, in this case it is you who are the thief, Françoise is the handkerchief, and Louis Perreyve is the miller of Montfort."

"Louis Perreyve a miller?"—in his puzzle he forgets to puff—"you mistake, Mademoiselle. I have been told that Monsieur Perreyve is in the army of the North."

"Listen to me"—she speaks sharply. "Before Louis went away he was betrothed to Françoise Gérard, in my presence—do you hear?—in my presence"—she calls this loudly, for Monsieur Constant has turned his face away from her observant eyes.

"I hear, Mademoiselle," and Louise softens when

she sees that tears are rolling over his round cheeks;
"but—but I have been cruelly treated"—there is a sob
in his voice.   "Should not Madame Gérard have told
me this?   I—I am attached to Mademoiselle Françoise,"—he puts his hand on his heart.

"And you knew nothing about Louis?"

"Mademoiselle"—he raises his head and puffs more
than ever—"for what do you take me? I am an honest
man, I tell you, and Madame Gérard has not behaved
like an honest woman."

"Ah, but she cannot; she is not honest, Monsieur.
Do you not know—I am afraid to say it aloud, it is too
terrible, stoop down again—she is"—in a loud whisper
—"a fourolle?"

She crosses herself as the word is uttered, and
Constant turns as white as ashes.

"How do you know—can it be proved?" he
whispers back.

"It could soon be proved.   I myself have seen her
go out at night when she thought all the world was in
bed, for when I was younger I learned my trade in a
house opposite hers.   No one knows her story, but you
know it is sin that makes women fourolles, Monsieur
Constant"—she crosses herself again—"and when she
has served her seven years to the Evil One she will be

free, unless some one puts out her light. Ma foi, I would do it cheerfully if I could only meet her."

Constant gets paler still, and draws himself farther from the excited dressmaker.

"Mademoiselle," he puffs, "I wish you good-day— you must pardon me—but a man cannot be cheerful who in a few moments has had the happiness of his life destroyed. Oh!"—he burst into a yell of despair, shook the reins of his horse, and went off at a gallop.

CHAPTER III.

THE EX-CORPORAL MEETS HIS MATCH.

"MADAME LE GROS, come here, if you please, I have a commission for you."

Eustache has stood looking after Louise, his cap in one hand and his yellow handkerchief in the other, for nearly ten minutes. He is not quick at comprehension, but the dressmaker's words have stirred him strongly, and he casts about for the explanation of her warning. If she knows that Françoise wants looking after, others may know it too. "Mille tonnerres! I must do my duty to Louis, poor boy. Ah! why did he tie himself up so young?"

He remembers the bundle under his arm, and he comes down to the entrance of the washing-shed, and calls for Madame Le Gros.

A tall thin woman, her face hidden by the large pink kerchief tied over her cap, comes up from the water, rubbing her sinewy arms with her apron.

"Your servant, Mr. Corporal what do you want of me?"—among the women, with whom he is a favourite, Eustache is still Monsieur le Caporal.

As Madame Le Gros speaks, an idea comes into his head.

"Ma foi!" he says, " it is wonderful that I should have come here; among such a party of gossips, some one must know why Françoise wants to be taken care of."

But it is one thing to get an idea and quite another to be able to use it, and all Eustache does is to gaze earnestly in the face of the tall skinny washer-woman and hand her his bundle.

"Thank you, Monsieur, is that all I can do—tenez! What ails Monsieur this morning?"

Her sharp wits are puzzled by the corporal's grave face, for Eustache has always a smile and a joke for a woman.

"Hold!" he says, for she looks over her shoulder

as if meditating a return to her soaping; "yes, yes, I have it; Madame, my good neighbour, have you lately seen the young girl named Françoise Gérard?"

"Dame—I should think so. Françoise is not one of those who keep shut up within four walls."

"She is not ill, then?"—it has occurred to him that Louise's words may point to this meaning.

"Ill? no. Why should she be ill?" Madame Le Gros looks mocking and inquisitive.

"I do not know." Eustache feels foiled, and stares at the washerwoman till she laughs in his face

"Well"—he speaks angrily—"a girl frets after a lover sometimes, when he is away."

Madame Le Gros sets both her arms akimbo, and shakes her head.

"Ta—ta—ta, Françoise is not that sort—one goes another comes. She'll never marry Louis; ma foi, no."

Eustache frowns fiercely, and as she turns back to her washing, he grasps her arm.

"Say what you mean—I'm tired of the hints you women fling at one another. What do you mean? Who has Françoise put in my son's place?"

He roars like a bull, and his face is very red; and first one and then another of the capped and kerchiefed washers look over their shoulders as they kneel beside the Rille—then they gabble fast to one another ; and then, as Madame Le Gros answers, a buzzing chorus echoes her words—

"Monsieur Emile Constant of the mill at Montfort."

"Constant ?   I don't know him.   What is he like ?" says the ex-corporal, twirling his grey moustaches and looking as fierce as a wolf.

They all laugh—not at him, but at his question.

" He is a pudding "—"a ball "—"one of his own flour-sacks "—"he is more like a pair of bellows," Madame Le Gros screams till her voice tops the rest.

" He will be in town to-day for the market," says Eustache, and the women think he looks bloodthirsty.

" Well, Monsieur " — Le Gros pats him on the shoulder—"don't be too hard on the poor little man ; he can't help being rich, and a rich man to Thérèse Gérard is like a peach to a wasp."

"Bah !"   Eustache breaks away from her—he burns to meet this rival, this traitor, who steals another man's betrothed in his absence.   His plan is to await him in the market-place, where Constant is sure to be pointed out to him by the bystanders.

" Mother Thérèse !   What does it matter about Mother Thérèse ?—the man knows what he is about."

It is early yet, and there are few buyers on the

Place. The sellers are still busy putting up their booths, the corn-market is at one end under shelter, and although there seems to be an array of sacks but few of the owners have arrived.

Eustache looks about him uneasily—a hand touches his arm, and he hears the gasping voice of Madame Gérard. She usually avoids him, to-day she greets him with a sweet smile.

"Ah," he says, without answering her greeting, "you will do as well as any one ; look among those men yonder "—he points to the corn-market—" and tell me if one of them is Emile Constant, the miller of Montfort."

Thérèse gives a little start, for she sees how fiercely he glares at her, but she answers quietly—

" No, he is not there—at least I think not, for in truth I know little of him ; but, Monsieur Perreyve, what business can you have with the miller of Montfort ?"

Her look of simple surprise puzzles him.

" Well, Madame "—he takes off his cap and wipes his hot face with his handkerchief—" you know better than I do, perhaps. I have a reckoning to settle with this miller, and if you like you can stay and hear me call him to account for trying to come between my son and your daughter."

T

He holds **his** head angrily erect, and towers like a storm-cloud over the round, waddling woman.

Her face beams placidly, but the little bead-like eyes are very restless. She does not answer directly— she has not dreamed that Louise would carry out her threat so soon.

At last she says pleasantly—

"Come, come, Monsieur Perreyve, why should we quarrel? Monsieur Constant will not be here for an hour. Come home with me, and I will explain to you all I know of the matter, and you can talk to Françoise; believe me I am on your side."

Eustache believes in women—he always, when he can choose between the sexes, prefers to blame a man, and now as he has time to spare, he thinks he will go with Madame Gérard—her house being so near the corn-market—and hear what she has to say.

She opens her house-door, waddles to the stair-foot, and calls for Françoise. No answer comes.

"I am sorry, Monsieur Perreyve," she says politely. "Françoise must have gone out in my absence; but if you will take the trouble to sit down, I can, I believe, tell you the state of the case." She sits down and gasps, but Eustache stands sullenly upright. "Monsieur Emile Constant," she wheezes, "has eyes in his head, and he sees how handsome the child is. I suppose neighbours see him look at her—doubtless they see him pay me visits. But, Monsieur, when I say to Françoise, 'Thou must not encourage Monsieur Constant,' she answers—for the child is quite innocent of harm—'Why not, mother; thou dost not think Louis would be jealous of a silly little ball of a man like the miller. Louis would laugh at him.'"

Eustache frowns.

"I will wait and see Françoise, Madame; you call it innocence, I call it coquetry, for a girl to trifle with one man when she belongs to another—especially when the new man is rich."

"Oh, Monsieur"—Thérèse smiles and pats his arm—"remember a handsome girl is like a flower, she takes all the sunshine and gives none back. You need not fear Françoise; make yourself easy and trust to me."

But while she smiles up at him there is such evil in her eyes that Eustache, spite of himself, doubts more than ever.

"No," he says impetuously; "that's just what I can't do. I can't feel easy till I've told that confounded miller to keep his eyes to himself. So by your leave Madame, I'll go back to the market and wait for him."

"Imprudent fool, he brings it on himself;" her eyes gleam fiercely, then she says aloud, carelessly, "Well, Monsieur, do as you please; but Françoise will grieve to have missed you. She was talking of you this morning; she shall be so proud of her tall, handsome father, she says."

Eustache leaves off frowning.

"Did she say so, little rogue?" and he strokes his moustache complacently. "Well, Madame, you will say to her that she might sometimes come and see me —she is always welcome."

"Ah, Monsieur, the poor child; how could she be sure of that when you were so determined that the marriage should be put off? But your message will make my Françoise quite gay. Come, Monsieur, before you go let us drink a glass to the success of our son Louis in the army of the North."

Eustache has two weaknesses—his own good looks and cognac, and Mother Thérèse knows them both. She has only one bottle and a few glasses inside the tall oak cabinet with the Venetian goblets at top, but she fumbles as if she were choosing from a store as her head disappears behind the carved open door.

She emerges presently with a small round black bottle and two glasses; she pours the liquor into these on the top of the cabinet, and then offers one to Eustache and puts her lips to the other.

The ex-corporal smacks his lips. "Mille tonnerres, Madame, but this is good, good, good"—his eyes stray to the bottle as he sets down his empty glass.

"Ma foi, Monsieur"—her restless eyes might have warned Eustache if his eyes had not been fixed on the bottle—"we are a clever pair. Between us we have forgotten to drink the health of our son Louis—permit me."

She sets his glass on the cabinet and bends over it while she fills it.

"To the health of our son—our dear son, Louis." She closes her eyes, and again she just tastes the brandy.

Eustache tosses his off; presently he looks at her with a dazed, foolish expression. He makes a step forward, and tries to speak, but only mumbles, and catches at the sofa to save himself from falling.

"Take my arm," says, Madame Gérard, "there is no time to lose, my friend. We will go and find Monsieur Constant."

Eustache takes her arm, but he puts out his other hand and reels against the wall of the passage.

"Gently—gently," Madame gasps, but her eyes

are keen as a knife till she has guided him safely out of the house and across the empty street into an archway a little further down, where there is a heap of empty wine-barrels.

He does not speak ; he follows her guidance blindly, and indeed his eyes are half-closed, and he leans on her so heavily that she can hardly walk beneath his weight. As soon as she gets behind the barrels she stops.

"Lie there, meddling fool," and she pushes him with all her strength.

He rouses, makes a clutching grasp, and, missing her, falls heavily on the round paving stones of the yard.

CHAPTER IV.

THE FOUROLLE MAKES ANOTHER CONQUEST.

THÉRÈSE'S flat round face peeps out of the archway, the street is empty, and she goes back to her house. In her hurry, for she knows the power of the dose she has given, and feared lest Eustache should fall in the room, she left the glasses on the table, and though she is hurrying to see Monsieur Constant, she goes in to remove these witnesses of her interview with the ex-corporal.

She opens the door and goes in. Standing at the entrance to the parlour, looking into the room, is Louise Courbon.

She turns quickly, and Thérèse sees how pale her face is.

"You are out early this morning, Madame," says the dressmaker; "have you seen Monsieur Constant?" —for the thought that comes to Louise as her quick eye lights on the wine-glasses is that the matter is already settled, and that Françoise has been that morning betrothed to the miller of Montfort.

Thérèse's eyes work strangely, and she too turns pale.

"Why should I see Monsieur Constant?" she says. "What does the girl mean?"

"I mean this, Madame. I told you I would do nothing sly, and to-day I have told Monsieur Emile that your daughter is promised to Louis Perreyve."

Through her half-closed lids she looks keenly at the old woman, but Thérèse's face is smoother than it was before.

"Magpies must chatter, it is their nature," she says calmly. "I should not dream of telling my private affairs to a stranger."

"Though you give a drop to 'a stranger' at this time of day," says the freckled woman with stinging emphasis. "Good day, Mother Thérèse, I may chatter, but I am not a will-o'-the-wisp."

Thérèse reddens, but she wants to be rid of her visitor, and so lets her depart unanswered ; then she hastily puts away the wine-glasses into the cabinet, and takes her way to the market.

The place is thronged, but scarcely any one greets Thérèse. The Curé of St. Ouen as he passes avoids the chance of speaking to her.

"Did you see ?' 'says old Nanon, the potato-seller, to Julie, the vendor of red cabbage and carrots close by, "Monsieur le Curé passes Thérèse Gérard without a word."

"*Mon Dieu !*" and gossiping red-haired Julie clasps her hands in horror, and repeats to her next neighbour that old Nanon saw Monsieur le Curé sign himself as he passed Mother Thérèse, because she is a fourolle.

"She ought to be burned or drowned," says the next neighbour Rose, and she goes home and tells her husband that Monsieur le Curé of St. Ouen says Thérèse Gérard ought to be burned or drowned for being a will-o'-the-wisp.

Monsieur Constant is busy among the corn-merchants at the farther end of the market, but he sees Thérèse on her way towards him.

He too turns his back on her, and screws his round flat face into a listening expression as he plucks the sleeve of the slowest speaker in Pont-Audemer, Monsieur Ricanot, the tailor, and asks him the news of the day.

But Thérèse sees this manœuvre and understands it. She can be as patient as a camel when she has a point to gain. So she hovers round the unhappy little man, like the fourolle people say she is, till at last the corn-merchants drop away one by one, and he is left alone.

Then, as if she just perceived him, she darts on him with the sudden descent of a hawk.

"Ah, good day, my friend, and you are coming to see us, are you not, as you promised?"

She turns as if to walk beside him to her house, but Emile retreats.

His round face has become a very greasy yellow, and his eyes stare duller than ever.

"Madame must excuse me," he stammers. "I have to return home early, and I must forego the honour of the visit"

Thérèse laughs till the tongue shows in her empty mouth.

"What a pity," she says, "when Françoise has

stayed in all the morning to have the chance of thanking you for the charming flowers. Well, then, you must give me a pretty message for my daughter ;" she nods her head triumphantly, though she is wondering how to get this fat idiot—as she calls him—home, and settle the matter irrevocably.

"Her daughter !" Constant's lower jaw drops, and he looks ready to faint with terror. Thérèse gazes at him with such astonished glances that he is forced to speak. "Madame—I have been told news—Madame —why did you not tell me that your daughter was not free, that she was promised to Louis Perreyve ?"

He clenches both fists in the energy of his demand, for at the remembrance of the deception practised on him he thinks only of losing Françoise, and forgets his fear of the fourolle.

"Louis Perreyve !" Thérèse opens her little eyes. "Ma foi ! is there then no end to the gossip of Pont-Audemer ? Now, Monsieur," she says with an offended air, "I will wager that the teller of that news was a little freckled, green-eyed chatterbox called Louise Courbon, with a face like a toad and a tongue like a magpie. Tell me it was she, and you set my heart at rest."

Constant's dull wondering eyes stare at Madame Gérard.

"It was undoubtedly such a person, Madame ; I was about to make other inquiries, but somehow I was prevented."

He had nearly said, "If I could have got out of your sight or hearing I should have asked further questions, but now——" "But, Madame," he goes on, "I cannot see why this person should have come out to seek me and tell me what is not true."

Thérèse smiles till her brick-dust face is full of creases, and her eyes are less restless as she sees his anxiety for her answer.

"How good you are !" she gasps ; "how unsuspecting ! Why, Monsieur, the last time I saw Louise Courbon she told me that a rich man had taken the mill at Montfort, and that she would be his wife before the year was out, even if she had to ask him herself. It was that made me guess none but she could have made up such a story about my poor slandered child."

She rubs her hard, dry little eyes with the back of her hand, pretending not to see the rapid changes that pass over Constant's round stupid face.

"Good day, Monsieur," she goes on ; "I will tell Françoise that you care so little for her good name that you listen and give credit to the first tale-bearer you meet with.   What right had you to win my beautiful child's heart and then deceive her ?"

Constant stretches out both hands imploringly. "Her heart, did you say, Madame?" he puffs out. "Ah, mon Dieu! if I could hope—listen, Madame" —for Thérèse has turned her back on him and is departing. "I am not handsome, but I have a heart, and I am honest ; if this story is false, then I ask your pardon a thousand times, and I entreat you not to betray me to your charming daughter. Madame, I have shown my admiration for that young lady—but," he lays his fat hand on his heart, " my love is unspeakable—it is here—here !"—he slaps his chest several times—" and it consumes me." Thérèse has turned round, and is looking at him steadily, but he is too much excited to notice her gaze. " Madame"—he waves both hands—" when I heard that that fair enchanting creature had belonged to another man before I saw her, and that while still belonging to him she had smiled on me as she has done, and led me to hope for success, I felt as if—as if I should burst—you might have put me into the mill and ground me into flour. No, Madame, I am not handsome, but deception I cannot forgive."

Again Thérèse's eyes grow restless.

"Well, Monsieur, I forgive you, and if you will promise not to listen to any more idle gossip, I will let you see Françoise, and bring matters to a conclusion, for it seems to me that is what you want."

"Madame, you are too good," he says. "I left home with this intention, and if I had not met that freckled mischief-maker I should this morning have asked for the hand of your daughter."

Thérèse waves her hand impatiently. "Do not speak of that girl Louise. She shall never make another gown for me—never. Since you wish it, let us go and find Françoise."

"What is the old witch doing with the foolish-faced miller?" says red-haired Julie to old Nanon.

"She has cast a spell on him," says that withered old dame; "and he will fade like a summer flower."

CHAPTER V.

THE MILLER SPEAKS HIS MIND.

EVENING draws on, and the lull which has come over the little town since the bustle of the market departed is broken now by the sound of the fife and drum, and the steady tramp-tramp of a body of soldiers as they pass through the town on their way to Honfleur. They may only halt for half an hour or so, but two or three privates whose homes are in the town have leave to stay and greet their friends, and join the regiment at Havre.

As they pass her door, Mother Thérèse looks out in the dusk. She can only see the soldiers moving at a quick pace.

"Curse the red-coated fools," and she closes the door, rejoicing that Françoise stays within.

Soon after a tall man staggers out of the archway and comes into the street; he goes a little way down it, and then, feeling giddy, he seats himself on a door-step, nearly opposite Thérèse's house, and falls asleep.

The street seems to have gone to rest, when all at once hurried steps come from the end near the little bridge. A tall young soldier walks at a fast pace, and behind him lags the watchman of Pont-Audemer with his huge horn lantern.

"Pouf!" says this worthy, "I can't keep up with your long legs, Louis—we have been to every drinking-shop in the town—go home to bed, your father will turn up safe and sound in the morning."

But the young soldier has seen the sleeping man and stops beside him, and as the lantern is turned on his face they both recognise Eustache.

"Ciel!" exclaims Louis, "what has happened? It is my father, he is not drunk, he is ill—what do I know, dying? help me, my friend."

They raise Eustache and drag him between them, but they do not take him home; instead, Louis stops at the door of Louise Courbon's house, and knocks loudly.

"I have found him," he says to the dressmaker; "But something terrible has happened—see how his head has been bleeding."

They get the doctor, and they watch beside him all night; but Eustache does not regain consciousness.

At last, as morning steals into the room, he opens his eyes.

"Louis"—he does not seem surprised to see his son—"you need not take care of Françoise—the witch will kill you if you meddle—let her marry the miller if she likes."

He closes his eyes again, and is deaf to all questions.

Louise grows white.

"Mon Dieu!" she whispers, "had Eustache been drinking with her yesterday morning, and has she poisoned him?"

And then she tells Louis the events of the previous day.

An hour later Louis Perreyve knocks at Madame Gérard's door.

He respects Louise—he knows she is true, but he thinks she is prejudiced against Thérèse, and he cannot give up his trust in Françoise.

The girl opens the door herself—Louis enters quickly and clasps her in his arms.

She struggles away from him.

" No, Monsieur ; no, Louis—you must not—mother ! oh, mother, come here !"

The young soldier lets her go and then stands stupefied while Thérèse waddles out of the back room, where she is making coffee.

" Monsieur Perreyve, this is an unexpected honour," she gasps contemptuously.

" What do you mean, Madame ?"—his senses are coming back to Louis, and with them comes violent anger.

" I mean that when a man is dolt enough to listen to his father and to go for a soldier, when he might marry the girl he loves, he deserves to lose her. Your father was rich enough to buy you a substitute, Louis Perreyve. If you wouldn't stay to take care of Françoise you have no right to her. She is now another man's property."

" Hold your tongue, shameless woman," he says

fiercely ; " if my father were still rich, you would not dare to play me false." He checks himself, and turns to Françoise. " My beloved," he says tenderly, " I do not wrong you by a doubt : you are true—you love me —and you will not listen to your mother's words ?"

" My mother says the truth—I am not true to you." Françoise blushes and hangs her head. " There has been deceit enough, but I meant to write and tell you to-day."

" You are not true—heavens !"—he snatches her hands and compels her to raise her eyes. " Mon Dieu ! can you be false—you whom I have so trusted ? Françoise—look at me—look into my heart and say you do not love me."

The girl blushes redder still, her lips quiver, and she shrinks from him in a burst of tears.

" Oh, mother—mother—you promised to spare me this "—she clasps her hands over her eyes. " I said I could go through with it all—if I did not see Louis—I cannot bear it."

Louis tries to put his arm round her, but she pushes him away.

Mother Thérèse has stood looking at them with her restless eyes. She stamps her foot, and draws Françoise to her.

U

"You fool"—she shakes the girl's arm—"you poor whining fool!" she gasps. "You will then marry this poor soldier, and give up all your fine prospects?"

Françoise shakes herself free—she raises her head and looks calmly at Louis.

"You think yourself very clever, mother," she says, "and you like to call names, but you are wrong, though I shall marry to please myself, not you." She looks at Thérèse, and laughs at the alarm in her face.

"Louis," she says, "do not try to win me back. I esteem you too much to listen to you: you cannot make me happy." Then, as he turns away in anger— "Listen, my friend, only a rich man can make me happy. If I marry you I shall only love you a little while—as soon as hardships begin I shall hate you and leave you."

"Françoise"—he stretches out his hands imploringly —"it is not your own self who speaks. Think how happy we have been—think how I love you; ah, you do not know how happy I can make you my beloved— come back to me, my Françoise."

But the girl still shrinks back, and Thérèse stands between the lovers.

"This must be ended, Monsieur," she says; "you must be thought of as well as Françoise. My daughter dares not listen. She promised herself yesterday to Monsieur Emile Constant, the miller of Montfort."

"Is this true?" Louis speaks vehemently, then, pushing past the old woman, he drags Françoise to the stairs' foot, where there is more daylight than in the narrow entrance passage. "Who is this man?" he looks at her sternly; "I never heard of him. Speak—do you love him?"

"Let me go"—Françoise is wild with grief and anger—"he is not a stranger—yes, my mother has told you the truth."

As she speaks there is a loud knocking at the door. Thérèse turns a gray paleness, she is so frightened that she stands helpless, leaning against the passage wall. Louis lets go of Françoise and opens the door.

Side by side, looking as strange a pair as could be seen, are Louise and Monsieur Constant.

The miller's large dull eyes are full of angry excitement; but Louise is radiant. She glances over the group in the passage, and then she turns to her companion.

"Well, Monsieur, do you believe me now?" Then speaking to the astonished group, "Why do you all stand here?" says the brisk little woman; and she goes into the parlour, the others following like a flock of sheep.

"Now, Monsieur Constant, you have to excuse yourself to my friend Louis, and let the blame fall where it is really due."

The miller, thus exhorted, holds up his flat round head and prepares to puff out his words with extra vigour ; but Louis stands stupefied by surprise that stifles anger.   He turns slowly from the heavy unmeaning face and unwieldy figure to Françoise, but she will not meet his eyes.   Till now she has braved it out— she has conquered the longing she had for Louis's love —from very fear of her own weakness she has kept firm, but she cannot bear his contempt, she cannot bear him to see the man she has put in his place—she turns away as the miller speaks, and hides her face against the wall.

" Mademoiselle Courbon, when I called on her this morning," he says pompously, "when I questioned her this morning on some information she gave me yesterday—said I should find Monsieur Perreyve here, and that I owed him an explanation."   He does not look at Louis ; he directs his discourse to the Venice goblets, which come precisely into level with his staring eyes.   "But I do not feel that I owe explanation or anything to anybody.   Morbleu ! shall I give explanations when I have been deceived, made a fool of—what do I say, outraged ?" he screams out with sudden wrath, and shakes both fists in the face of Madame Gérard.

She rouses with an effort, for the sight of Louise has paralysed her with terror. Thérèse's first thought was that Eustache had denounced her—but the dressmaker's silence gives her hope that as yet nothing has been discovered.

"Monsieur Constant," she says, "a promise cannot be broken—you are the promised husband of my child : pay no heed to these fables—look at Françoise and do not listen to these intruders."

"No, I will not look at her, traitress," he screams in fury. "Ah, hag, harpy, murderess, for have you not nearly murdered the father of this gentleman ? Marry your daughter ! do you think I could be sure of my life, you witch ? Take yourself away, infamous that you are—take yourselves both away from Pont-Audemer, or I will have you prosecuted and punished. Monsieur "—he turns suddenly to the young soldier— " shake hands, Monsieur, we are well rid of such a wife —come—come away as you would from the pit of hell—and you Mademoiselle "—to Louise—" open the door, if you please."

Eustache recovered after a while from the effects of the narcotic he had swallowed, and from the injuries he had received in his fall.

His son went back to the army of the North, reckless what became of him ; and the Gérards disappeared in the night from Pont-Audemer. Gossips say that the Evil One fetched away his own ; and gossips also say that soon afterwards the miller of Montfort proposed to the little dressmaker. but that she prefers to remain Mademoiselle Louise Courbon.

CHAPTER XII.

CAUDEBEC—ROUEN—ST. ROMAIN AND THE DRAGON—"A WAIF OF THE WOODS"—CHÂTEAU GAILLARD.

FROM Pont-Audemer one must cross the Seine to reach Caudebec.

Perhaps one of the most charming sights the Seine offers to the traveller who comes down the river in the little steamer from Rouen to Havre is the pretty town of Caudebec, backed by richly wooded hills, with its broad terrace beside the river, along which a double avenue of trees runs close to the water's edge ; while behind, above the quaint half-timbered houses, rise the rich spires of the fine church—or cathedral, as travellers so often call it. We reached Caudebec on market-day, and the broad quay was alive with country folk, who not only set up their stalls here but spread the ground with their merchandise, while their lofty green-hooded waggons stood ranged under the tall trees of the avenue. But the market was at its best in the Grande Place in front of the church, and this is altogether the most picturesque sight to be seen in either Normandy or Brittany, not even excepting

MARKET-PLACE, CAUDEBEC.

the market of Quimper; for although the Breton costumes are far more rich in colour and quaint in form than the ordinary Norman peasant clothing, the Caudebec women get the pull in the taste with which they display their wares, and in the far greater charm of the Place itself.

Henri Quatre said the grand old church at one end of this Place was the finest chapel he had ever seen ; its southern side completely fills the end of the square, the other three sides of which are filled by quaint old fifteenth-century houses, as yet but little modernised. Hitherto Caudebec has been a sleepy town, full of old-world quiet, only broken by the noise of the bark mills which at times make the whole place unsavoury ; the railway is some miles off, and the demon Improvement has not yet cast his eyes on this rarely picturesque town beside the silver Seine, with its gray fringe of willows and its winding curves ; but he is not far off —it is only a question of months, or perhaps a year or two. The traveller who would see this perfect speci-men of an old Norman town, still wearing the picturesque charm that old age gives, and with all the freshness of old-world ways still clinging to its people, should visit it without delay. There is plenty of sketching to be done in the town, and the walks are lovely.

Sauntering on beyond the avenue, along the dusty white road, now shaded by a lofty tree-covered hill, where old Norman farm-houses nestle, now screened from the river by wan phantom-like birches, we came one afternoon to the exquisite little pilot village, Villequier, with its tiny-spired church perched half-way up the wooded height, as if it would keep its distance alike from the castle above and the cottages at its feet. This village, where the river curves in an exquisite bay, is a station for the pilots who guide boats and barges through the perils of the Seine and its dreaded Barre.

The large illustration shows the principal street of Caudebec, lined with old houses. At the end rises the richly carved church spire, which, like the rest of the building, is a miracle of stonework. We spent some time in this delightful little town, and were very unwilling to leave its peaceful beauty for the more noisy and crowded city of Rouen.

Rouen.

THE city of Rouen has been so well and so exhaustively described by so many writers that it does not seem necessary to give any detailed account of it in this book. Only a few years ago it was the most picturesque city of Normandy, perhaps, indeed, of Europe ; now, alas, much of its quaint originality has disappeared, and the old houses that remain are being

GRANDE RUE, CAUDEBEC.

replaced by modern inanities, the old streets will soon

AN OLD COURT IN ROUEN.

have passed away, and only the churches and a few
public buildings will remain of old Rouen.   Even

public buildings have been deprived in a large measure, owing to these changes, of their picturesque connecting links with the past.

The Place de la Vieille Tour is perhaps the least modernised of the old Places of Rouen; it still possesses many picturesque points. The building called Monument Saint Romain stands in this Place, opposite the Halle aux toiles or Cloth Market; it is a picturesque specimen of the Renaissance style. This building is associated with a strange ancient custom, called La Levée de la Fierté de St. Romain; for on the top of the double flight of steps the Chapter of the cathedral, every year on Ascension Day, was entitled to pronounce by one of their number the pardon of a criminal under sentence of death. How this privilege came to be accorded to the chapter of Rouen Cathedral the following legend will show :—

Saint Romain and the Dragon.

SAINT ROMAIN had passed his youth at the court of Clotaire the Second, and was loved and reverenced by rich and poor alike for his piety and modesty. He was consecrated bishop of Rouen about 630, and he at once vigorously set to work to put down idolatry. His pious efforts were crowned with great success and he had power given him to work miracles. The most famous among these exploits was his encounter with a dragon called Gargouille. An enormous monster of this species suddenly appeared in a marshy meadow in the neighbourhood of Rouen, and very soon the creature filled the hearts of the townspeople with sorrow and dismay; he devoured indiscriminately all the men, women, children, and animals who came in his way. No one dared venture near the marsh, and all business which lay beyond the town on that side was suspended. This wholesale destruction of his flock greatly troubled St. Romain, and he turned over in his mind many ways of putting an end to Monsieur Gargouille's inordinate appetite. At last he determined to make a direct attack upon the monster. He announced his intention in the cathedral, and expressed a desire that some one should accompany him on the expedition. But no one seemed inclined to accept the privilege. At last the bishop's difficulty came to the ears of a criminal under sentence of death, and he at once offered his services. The bishop accepted them gladly, and the two set forth for the marsh. St. Romain only took his pastoral staff; but his companion preferred to carry a serviceable sword and shield.

When the monster saw the saint and the sinner approaching he rushed towards them, flapping his huge wings, and, making a fearful outcry, he spat forth fire from his mouth and nostrils.   The criminal felt his last hour was come, but put himself in an attitude of defence.   Nothing daunted by the fearful sight, the good bishop instinctively raised his hand and made the sign of the cross, uttering a sentence in very good ecclesiastical Latin.   To the bishop's surprise—for it must be owned he was feeling more confidence in the effect of a good blow from his staff than from any Latin—the dragon instantly dropped his blustering attitude, and cowered before his adversaries.   The bishop without more ado whipped off his stole, passed it round the monster's neck, and delivering him to the criminal, bade him lead the dragon into the city.

Great was the wonder of the inhabitants when they saw the trio approach—the bishop walking beside the dragon as calmly as if he were pacing the cathedral, and Monsieur Gargouille shambling along with lowered crest and drooping wings, held in leash by the criminal ; and so, followed by the rejoicing townsfolk, they passed on to the cathedral square, where Monsieur Gargouille, by the order of the bishop, was tied to a stake and burned.

It need hardly be said that the condemned criminal received a free pardon for his share in the exploit.

MONUMENT TO ST. ROMAIN, ROUEN.

In order that the memory of this great miracle might be preserved, the king Dagobert gave to the cathedral of Rouen the power to pardon every year, at Ascension tide, a criminal under sentence of death. The pardon was pronounced from the top of the double staircase, and then the criminal walked in a procession of priests and acolytes to the cathedral, carrying la Fierté de St. Romain.　La Fierté was the casket containing the relics of St. Romain, and during the ceremony of his pardon the criminal was obliged to support this on his shoulders.　This curious custom was only done away with at the time of the Revolution.

Many quaint by-streets and lanes still exist in Rouen ; the illustration represents one of these.

All sorts of legends are told of Rouen and the neighbouring country ; a very popular one is related of Richard the Fearless, third Duke of Normandy, whose father and grandfather, William Longsword and Rollo, are both buried in Rouen cathedral.

A Waif of the Woods.

A LEGEND OF DUKE RICHARD THE FEARLESS.

> " A Richard le Normant aduint maintes merveilles
> Vers celles que vueil dire elles sont nompareilles
> Quon puis dire de bouche ne escouter doreilles."
>
> *Roman de Richart.*

PART I.

ONE evening, just after sundown, Richard, Duke of Normandy, called Sans Peur, was riding slowly through the wood near his chateau de Molineaux. As he passed under the branches of a lofty tree he heard the wailing cries of an infant. He stopped his horse and listened —the cries redoubled, and, to his astonishment, they seemed to come from above his head.

The Duke quickly dismounted, and, fastening his horse to a tree, began to unbuckle his spurs.

" Surely the child is in the tree," he thought ; " I will climb and find out."

Another burst of cries and sobs, and he began to climb the tree as fast as he could ; guided by the voice, he soon discovered the little creature niched in a hollow formed by two branches. Then he looked at his discovery. It was a beautiful child, and its clothes were

X

of a good fashion and texture.   As soon as the Duke touched it it left off crying.   He clasped it to his breast, and climbed down the tree carefully.

"Whose child can this be?" he said.   "By my faith, I must be its godfather, poor little soul."

The Duke tenderly wrapped it in his cloak and remounted his horse, then he rode quickly towards the cottage of his forester and knocked at his door.

"See what I have brought you, Margot," he said to the forester's wife.   "Your trees bear strange fruit."

He held the child to the woman, but it began to cry out loudly, and showed by its looks and movements that it wished to remain with the Duke.

"Holy Saints!" said Margot, "does my lord mean that he found this beautiful creature in the forest?"

"Yes, by my faith, I plucked it from a tree; how it got there the saints only know.   As I rode along I heard loud cries in the air; I climbed a tree, and this little apple was growing on a branch."

While the Duke spoke, Margot had got the little creature in her lap, and began to take off its clothes.

"Tell me, my good Margot," said the Duke, "is it a boy or a girl."

"By the blessed Virgin, my lord, it is the most beautiful girl that was ever made."

"That pleases me well," said Richard. "I put her in your charge, Margot ; you must be a mother to her."

"Yes, yes, Monseigneur, your will shall be obeyed."

The Duke put some gold pieces on the table and gave a parting kiss to the child, who laughed and crowed with delight ; then he mounted his horse and rode away.

It was now nearly dusk, and as the Duke turned into one of the wide alleys of the forest he came upon a large pack of hounds ; behind them ran the huntsmen, blowing horns, and after these came a great number of men on horseback.

The Duke's horse stood still and trembled in every limb.

But Richard cried out, "By the true God, I will know who are these who dare to hunt without my leave."

Suddenly the Mesgnie Hellequin[1] came into his mind, and just then he espied among the troop one of his own squires who had died a year ago. The Duke urged his trembling, stumbling horse towards the figure. "From whence do you come ?" he asked ; "what brings you here ? were you not the seneschal of my court ? and have you not been dead a year ?"

The phantom hunter and his troop. A superstition of Normandy.

"Yes, sire," said the figure, in a hollow voice, "I was seneschal of your court, and I died a year ago."

"Tell me then," said Richard, "how have you come to life again?"

"Alas, sire, I am not alive, I am a spirit, and I am doing penance for my sins, and so are all the rest you see here. We are all the servants of Hellequin."

"How dares he hunt in this forest without my leave," said the Duke angrily. "By the faith which I owe to God, I will not suffer it. Where is this Hellequin? I will learn from his own mouth who he is."

"Sire, you are my master, I will conduct you to him."

Then the squire led the Duke to a large thorn tree where a tall dark-looking man was seated. Richard the Fearless, as soon as he saw him, asked him by whose leave he hunted in the forest.

"By the leave of God," said the dark figure. He has commanded us to hunt in these woods all through the night. I am Hellequin."

Thus saying, Hellequin descended from the thorn tree, and seated himself upon a piece of silk which the seneschal had spread for him on the ground.

"Can you tell me, strange man, if I shall live long?" said Richard.

"I do not know, but I foresee that you will encounter many dangers ; however, neither friends nor enemies will have any power over you. Ask me nothing more. Farewell !"

Richard heard this prediction with great joy.

As he was going, Hellequin said, "Take this as a memento of our meeting," and he gave the Duke the rich piece of silk on which he had been sitting. The Duke bowed and returned to his horse. He threw the silk, which was of extraordinary richness and beauty, over the saddle, and laughed. "It will one day make a good robe for my foundling," he said.

PART II.

THE child throve fast and well under the care of the forester's wife. Indeed, her growth was almost magical, and each year that passed over her head seemed to increase her grace and beauty. Duke Richard, who was a bachelor, took the greatest interest in his protegée, and he paid constant visits to the cottage in the forest. He had kept this adventure a profound secret, and he had imposed silence on the child's foster-mother ; so the strange waif grew up like a sweet violet, lost to view in the shade of a wood.

One day after leaving the cottage, Duke Richard began to ask himself what would be the end of this affair, for he found that the beautiful girl was constantly in his thoughts, and that each time he saw her it was more difficult to leave her; in fact, the bold Duke was head over ears in love with his forest flower, not after the too frequent fashion of his order, but honestly in love. The maid was as modest as she was beautiful, but she could not help showing, by her delight whenever he appeared at the cottage, how tenderly disposed she was towards him.

"By my faith," said Richard, "it seems but the other day I carried her in my arms down the wood, and now she is a well-grown young woman. Margot has done her duty by her. Yes, yes; she is a beautiful creature, and without doubt would make a most loving and virtuous wife."

About this time the barons of Normandy, both great and small, held a consistory, and, as though they had divined their master's wishes, they resolved to ask him to choose a wife who might give him an heir to succeed in the government of the country; certain of their number therefore besought an interview with the Duke, and made known to him their desire with all due respect and formality.

Duke Richard smiled when he heard the request of his barons.

"By my faith," he said, "your desires jump with my own. I have been thinking of this very thing, and I am ready to do what you wish."

A chorus of pleasure was growled out by the barons, as they stroked their beards or twisted their moustaches, each man according to his habit.

"Sire," said the oldest and highest in rank, "there are several noble dames from whom we have thought your Grace might be pleased to choose."

"In the matter of choice," said the Duke, "I shall consult no one. I have in my mind a young maiden whose bringing up I have watched ever since she was a child. I could never find a maid more beautiful or more to my liking. She is young—but "—added the Duke with a smile, "she will grow older; I will make her my wife."

"Sire," said the barons, "may God give her on whom your heart is set the joy and honour of being your wife."

So the affair was settled, though, as you may suppose, a good deal of curiosity was excited by its singularity, and no question was asked so often as "Who is she?" especially among the ladies of the court, many of whom had hoped to be Duchess of Normandy. But it was all in vain, no one could get at the root of the mystery; the only person who could satisfy them was dumb; and, indeed, he knew no more of his protegée's parentage than they did. When the maiden appeared at court her wondrous grace and beauty, and her perfect modesty of demeanour, silenced all cavillers, and made clear to all that the Duke had sufficient excuse for his mysterious choice.

In due course the Archbishop of Rouen blessed the nuptials, which were celebrated with great magnificence in the Cathedral of Rouen; and the bride, in a robe made of the rare silk that Hellequin had given to the Duke, looked the most ravishing creature the world at that date had seen.

PART III.

FOR several years Duke Richard and his forest-bride lived happily together, the only drawback to their perfect bliss being that the desire of the duke and his barons for an heir was still unfulfilled. Duke Richard loved his wife so passionately he could hardly bear her to be out of his sight. He was always discovering in her fresh charms of mind and body—custom could not stale her infinite variety—her faults were almost virtues in his eyes ; even a strange mischievous grace and wilfulness that possessed her at times fascinated the bold duke.

But a sudden end came to all this happiness. One day the Duke found his wife lying on her bed—pale and spiritless ; a withering blight had fallen upon her ; he strove vainly to rouse her from this lethargy that dulled her faculties. At last she burst into tears.

"What ails you, sweet wife," said the Duke, much dismayed by her strange unusual mood.

"Sire," she said in a broken voice, "I am very ill ; I believe I am going to die."

"The holy saints forbid," cried the Duke.

A violent shudder passed over his wife at the words. "Alas, sire," she sobbed, "it is true ; I know I am going to leave you ; my strength and life seem passing away."

"My God ! it must not, cannot be," said the Duke, starting up. "A surgeon must see you at once."

"Richard, do not leave me," she said imploringly, laying her hand on his. "I am past all medicine, I feel death at my heart—while I can still speak listen to me—and I beseech you, by your love for me, grant me what I am going to ask."

"Speak, my soul's life ; I will do anything you wish."

" Sire, when I am dead "—her voice grew weaker and weaker—" let me be buried in the chapel in the middle of the forest where I was brought up ; and promise me, my dear lord, that you will watch during a whole night beside my coffin."

The Duke hid his face in his hands.   He could not speak, but the heaving of his shoulders told his anguish.

" Promise," said his wife, faintly.   The Duke raised his head ; he was very pale, and every feature was wrung with mental pain.

" If I have the misery, sweet wife, to see you dead, it shall be as you wish."

The Duchess was indeed past all help from the surgeons ; in a few hours from her seizure she lay pale and still as marble.   The Duke was inconsolable ; but, faithful to his promise, he ordered that the body of his wife should be taken in the evening to the chapel in the forest.   There, dressed in splendid robes of state, the body of the young Duchess was laid on a magnificent bier, surrounded by blazing torches.   The archbishop and his priests chaunted a solemn service for the dead, and recommended the soul of the Duchess to God.

The office finished, the clergy returned to Rouen ; but the Duke remained to fulfil his promise to his dying wife—to watch during the night beside her body. One knight only of his attendants, a loved and trusted friend, stayed to keep vigil with him.

Richard was very heavy hearted ; the joy of his life seemed to have gone from him. The whole thing had been so awfully sudden—it appeared like a hideous dream. He could not realise that his gay sweet wife was dead, that it was only her lifeless form he looked upon ; and as he gazed he fancied he saw a smile curving her beautiful lips, and he almost expected her to speak.

"Oh, my love, my wife," he cried, "speak to me ; say you are not dead—say you will come back to me in the morning light."

There was no answering voice ; only the echoes of the place returned his bitter cry ; but he seemed to hear strange whisperings in the air, and to feel the fluttering of wings around him.

The Duke raised his head and looked round the chapel.

"Heard you aught ?" he said to the knight beside him, who was white with fear.

"Yes, sire, strange mutterings, and sounds like wings beating the air."

"Some foul bird has got into the chapel," said the Duke ; and his head again sank on his breast.

Towards midnight Richard and his companion were seized with heavy sleep. Then a strange thing happened. The body of the Duchess struggled violently and raised itself on the bier—a terrible cry echoed through the forest. Richard started awake ; he felt no fear, he only loosened his sword in its sheath and placed it across his knees.

Then a voice from the bier, like the voice of his wife, cried out, " What ails you, Duke Richard. In all countries they tell of your daring. They say that from prime to compline you never fear any living person, and now behold your flesh quivers with terror. Come no nearer, Richard, do not touch me, or perchance I shall swoon again."

"What does this mean ?" cried the astonished Duke. "Are you my own wife ? were you not dead when they placed you on the bier to-day ? "

"No ; I had only swooned with violent thirst. Listen, if you truly love me, if you would have me alive again, do what I ask. At the entrance of the wood, as you know, there is a fountain of delicious water—fetch me some."

"I go, sweet wife," said Richard, and he instantly

left the chapel. But he had not gone many steps when a piercing cry came from the building. The Duke quickly retraced his steps ; the faithful companion of his watch lay lifeless on the floor of the chapel. The bier was empty ! A peal of mocking laughter rang through the air, and then a loud voice cried out—

"Ho! ho! Duke Richard, Brudenor has made a fool of you this time. I was your dearly-loved wife— I—Brudenor.[1] Ho! ho! ho!"

"Ah, wicked and deceitful creature," said the Duke. "I swear by the God who made me, that if ever you cross my path again, I will hew you in pieces with my sword."

Another peal of laughter, and all was still.

Richard carefully laid the body of his knight upon the bier, and watched beside it till the day broke.

When the hour of prime arrived, the archbishop and the priests returned to the chapel to chant the service over the body of the Duchess.

"Sing no more psalms for my wife, my Lord Archbishop. The great devils of hell have carried her away ;" and the Duke told the night's adventure.

The archbishop tried to comfort him.   "Do not

[1] An evil spirit called Brudenor seems to have played many tricks on Richard the Fearless.

fear or doubt my liege, we know that the devils have power both by night and by day to tempt Christians."

"Ah, my lord archbishop," interrupted Richard, bitterly, "but I have been so foully deceived. I swear by the splendour of heaven I will not take another wife for seven years or more."

And in order to keep his promise—after having buried his murdered knight with great pomp—Duke Richard shut himself up in his abbey of Fécamp, of which he was the founder, and remained there in seclusion.

We left Rouen one fine bright morning for Les Andelys ; we were to see the famous Hotel du Grand Cerf at Le Grand Andely, and also Château Gaillard, one of the most picturesque and remarkable castles in Normandy. The Château is placed on the Seine between Paris and Rouen, and the town of Le Petit Andely lies below the castle walls.

The ruin rises proudly from the summit of a lofty chalk cliff ; it is connected only on one side with the adjacent hills by a narrow tongue of land.

Richard Cœur de Lion in defiance of the treaty of Louviers, and to spite his rival Philip Augustus, built this famous castle. Tradition says Richard was his own architect. Delighted with his pet creation he called it his "saucy castle;" and it was begun and finished in one year. The Archbishop of Rouen excommunicated the lion-hearted king for building this fortress. The donjon, built in the form of an irregular circle, was of great strength. It contained the royal apartments;

CHÂTEAU GAILLARD.

the walls are more than fourteen feet thick. It is only reasonable to believe that this castle would have lasted intact till the present day if man had not destroyed his own handiwork. When Philip Augustus saw the "saucy castle," he swore by all the saints that he would "take it if it were made of iron." To which vaunting speech Richard made answer, "I would hold it if it were made of butter."

After the death of Richard, Philip besieged Château Gaillard. It withstood him for six months, and the garrison only surrendered under pressure of starvation.

With a garrison of one hundred and twenty men the castle afterwards withstood our Henry the Fifth for sixteen months, only yielding when water failed, owing to the wearing out of the ropes with which the buckets were sent down into the well.

Château Gaillard remained in a perfect state until 1606, when Henri Quatre dismantled it with other fortresses.

The view from the castle is very fine, commanding the lovely winding river for miles. It has been the prison of many celebrated criminals and prisoners, among them the unhappy Marguerite de Bourgogne, who is said to have been strangled in its vaults by the order of her husband Louis the Tenth.

THE END.